I0536194

LOVING LEO

A Strong Man's Hand - Book Five

KAT CARRINGTON

Published by Blushing Books
An Imprint of
ABCD Graphics and Design, Inc.
A Virginia Corporation
977 Seminole Trail #233
Charlottesville, VA 22901

©2021
All rights reserved.

No part of the book may be reproduced or transmitted in any form or by any means, electronic or mechanical, including photocopying, recording, or by any information storage and retrieval system, without permission in writing from the publisher. The trademark Blushing Books is pending in the US Patent and Trademark Office.

Kat Carrington
Loving Leo

eBook ISBN: 978-1-64563-947-3
Print ISBN: 978-1-64563-948-0
v1

Cover Art by ABCD Graphics & Design
This book contains fantasy themes appropriate for mature readers only.
Nothing in this book should be interpreted as Blushing Books' or
the author's advocating any non-consensual sexual activity.

Chapter 1

Shelby Beauchamp Davis looked over her notes once again. She was putting together the story of her grandmother's girlhood right here in Boone, Indiana, and she was finding the story fascinating. To look back and get a peek of what her grandparents' and great-grandparents' lives were like was something she'd wanted to do for a long time. Her grandmother, GG, was more than happy to pass down the history of their family in a way that made it so real. Shelby had laughed, she'd been shocked, and she'd cried at the story so far. Her Gran had had two brothers, whom Shelby had never gotten to know; she'd met her Uncle Carl a handful of times, but her Uncle Bryce had died unexpectedly at age forty-nine, so her Gran's stories were bringing them to life for her.

Shelby rubbed the small of her back and rested a hand on her pregnant belly. So far that morning, her baby had been active, as though he or she was growing eager to greet the world. It wouldn't be much longer now, and Shelby and her husband, Sam, were counting down the days. GG smiled at her and gave her belly a gentle pat.

"How's our little one today?"

"Trying to kick his way out, I think," Shelby said with a chuckle. "If this baby is as active after birth as before, we're going to have our hands full."

Shelby and GG settled down in the library in front of a comfortably crackling fire, each with a cup of tea. Shelby arranged her notebooks and other supplies and then gave her grandmother an eager smile. "Are you ready to go on with your story, Gran?"

GG gave her a wink. "I had a good night's sleep and a nice long dream about your grandfather, so, yes, I'm ready."

"Okay." Shelby leaned over and turned on the tape recorder. "Let's begin."

GG and Leo Beauchamp sat in the little Boone, Indiana church on Sunday morning, listening to the pastor speak to his congregation. Leo shifted a little and his leg pressed against his wife's leg. She felt an immediate rush of heat that went straight to her groin and her cheeks turned pink. She sat just as still as she could, trying not to think of the effect her husband's touch had on her. She nearly gasped with relief when the pastor asked them all to stand and sing a hymn. Leo was oblivious to her discomfort, she was glad to see, as she suspected that he might find it funny if he knew. Sometimes she wondered if the reactions of her body that had been unleashed on their wedding night were normal or if she was some kind of sex addict. And she *knew* her husband would find *that* funny. Her pink cheeks were not cooling off a bit and she threw her whole concentration into singing the hymn until she felt in control again. Until they were seated and she realized that her panties were just a little bit damp.

When the service was over, GG was sure the others around them could tell by looking at her what kind of inappropriate feelings were leaving her a little weak in the knees. She was seriously relieved that she had kept her coat with her instead of hanging it up. Leo helped her on with it and she gave him a bright smile. It took them a while to make their way through the congregation and finally out the door, after speaking to everyone they knew and shaking the pastor's hand. Once out of the church, GG heaved a huge sigh and said, "Wow! I'm glad we're out of there."

Leo gave her a puzzled look and said, "I thought you liked going to church."

Flustered, GG said, "Oh, I do…I just…never mind."

One of their friends called out to them just then and took Leo's attention away from what his wife was saying. The three of them talked for a couple of minutes and then GG and Leo went on to the parking lot and got into the car. They were going to Leo's parents' house for Sunday dinner, but they were going home to change clothes first and pick up the cake GG had made. They had settled into a routine of alternating weeks of Sunday dinners with their families. When they got home, Leo took GG's coat and pulled her close for a long kiss. She melted against him, immediately aroused, as always.

"Now what did you mean when you said you were glad to be out of church?" Leo asked.

"Geez, you never forget anything, do you?"

Leo laughed. "I try not to. Come on; spill it."

GG's cheeks were pink again. "I just…I had sort of a reaction. Leo, how can you make me want to have sex just by pressing your leg against mine? And in a place like church?"

Leo burst out laughing. "Well, I'm not sure, but I'm not complaining. In fact, I consider myself to be a lucky man!"

GG stared at him in disbelief. "Leo, we were in church! And I was sitting there getting turned on. There must be something blasphemous about that. Isn't there?"

Leo advanced on her with an evil grin. "Maybe we should do something about your shameful desires right now."

"Oh my gosh, we're going to your parents' as soon as we change clothes!"

He nuzzled her neck and said, "We can be a little bit late."

She tried to back away from him, but her traitorous body was melting under his hands. "Leo," she said weakly, "we shouldn't do this. And you didn't answer my question about being turned on in church."

Leo chuckled at her again and said, "Look, God created man and woman to give each other companionship and to procreate, right? That means God created the act of making love, right? So, it wouldn't be appropriate to be groping each other while we try to listen to the sermon, but your feelings are perfectly natural and given to you by God. Feel better?"

GG stared at him, unsure of exactly how serious his answer was. "Are you telling me the truth, or just trying to make me feel better?"

"It makes perfect sense to me. GG, there's nothing weird or abnormal about you having a healthy sex drive. In fact, it makes me love you even more if that's possible. But we should get changed and get to my parents' house. We'll take this up when we get back." He winked at her and let her go.

GG flashed her brilliant smile at him and scampered away to change her clothes. She was in her bra and panties when her husband came into the room and started to get out of his jacket and tie. The look he gave her was all it took to bring that rush of heat back over her body. She hurriedly pulled her jeans on and yanked a sweater over her head while he laughed at her. Leo walked toward her and she backed warily away, pointing her hairbrush at him until she realized he was just getting some casual clothes out of the dresser.

"I'm going to get my cake ready to go," GG said as she escaped from the bedroom.

Leo joined her in the kitchen a couple of minutes later and stopped to admire the pretty picture she made, setting her applesauce stack cake into a cake carrier and snapping it shut. She took his breath away every time he looked at her. And it wasn't just how she looked. He was utterly captivated by her spirit and her personality. She was impulsive and adventurous, as kind-hearted as it was possible to be. She was intelligent and endlessly curious, and she had a huge capacity for love and compassion. And, to top it all off, she was the sexiest woman he'd ever met. She was also stubborn, a bit spoiled, and willing to be sneaky to get what she wanted. She would grow out of those traits; he would help her along that path.

"Are we ready?" Leo asked.

GG gave him a smile and a nod and they were on their way. The house was full of the aroma of Claire's pot roast and GG's stomach growled at the tantalizing smells. There were hugs all around and Leo set about teasing his younger sisters while GG helped Claire in the kitchen. Charles was checking the TV listings, looking for the football game, even though he already knew. They all enjoyed a noisy dinner together, lively with conversation and laughter. They ate their fill, and then Claire and the girls cleared the table and GG carried her cake to the table. There were oohs and aahs all around and Claire gave a nod of approval at sight of the stack of thin layers of cake, each spread with GG's mother's homemade applesauce.

"It looks perfect, GG," Claire proclaimed.

GG had been nervous about making the cake. She'd never done one before, but she had both moms to advise her and it had turned out well. Now, if it tasted as good as it looked, she could be proud of it. Claire cut the cake and they passed the slices around the table. GG watched Leo, holding her breath as he took the first bite. He tasted, then chewed, and then closed his eyes and swallowed.

"GG, this cake is delicious!" He got up from his chair and

wrapped his arms around her in a bearhug. The rest of them erupted in laughter and cheers.

"Oh, thank God," GG said. "I was so scared I wouldn't get it right."

"No worries, darlin'! You can make me one of these for my birthday, as a matter of fact." Leo pulled her chair out for her and she sat down, beaming at the rest of them. There were more exclamations of approval over the cake and they all enjoyed their dessert. Charles even had a tiny second piece, claiming he still had a little coffee to finish and he really needed some cake to go with it.

The rest of the afternoon went by as usual, the ladies cleaning and loading the dishwasher, Leo and Charles taking out the garbage. The football game was on TV and the girls pulled out the Monopoly game, begging Claire and GG to play. After the game was over, they all said their goodbyes and Leo and GG headed for home. GG leaned her head on Leo's shoulder and they discussed the day as they made the short drive to their little house.

"What are your plans for tomorrow, baby?" Leo asked.

"I'm doing my grocery shopping after I get my morning chores done and Mom gave me a recipe for a beef stew that goes in the oven for several hours. Katie gets out of school early tomorrow and we're going to do our letters for the VA."

"You'll be busy. I'm taking a long lunch tomorrow because I have a job interview." Leo turned the corner onto their street.

"You do? An engineering job?" GG looked thrilled.

"Yep, entry level transportation engineering and they specified veterans preferred, with the proper education."

"Oh, Leo, that's just the kind of thing you want to do!"

"I know, it's one of the best prospects I've looked at so far. I have one of those feelings that this could be the one." Leo turned to smile at her as he put the car in park in the driveway. GG threw her arms around his neck and gave him a heartfelt kiss. Leo kissed her back and said, "Let's take this in the house, baby."

They went in, and as soon as the door closed behind them, they were in each other's arms, leaving the cake carrier right there at the front door. GG giggled as Leo ferociously growled while he nibbled at her neck and earlobe. He cupped her bottom in his hands and lifted her off the floor and she responded by wrapping her legs around him. A moment later, he tumbled her onto the bed and kicked off his shoes before joining her there. His mouth plundered hers while he slid his hands up under her sweater and cupped her breasts in his hands. He could feel the hard nubs through the lacy bra she wore and rubbed his thumbs over them, making her gasp in response. GG sat up so he could pull the sweater off over her head, leaving her long, dark hair tumbled around her shoulders. Leo drank in the sight of her, her lips swollen and her eyes dark with desire. He never got tired of looking at her and she bent her head a little, casting him a sultry look and slipping one bra strap down over her shoulder.

Leo chuckled and murmured, "You naughty little thing, you know what you're doing to me, don't you?" Her response was to slip the other strap down and cross her arms protectively under her breasts.

Breathing faster, Leo reached out and stroked the rounded mounds of her breasts, gently working his fingers under her arms until he could circle one engorged nipple between his finger and thumb. GG sucked in her breath, her eyes going even darker. Leo reached behind her with his other hand and unfastened the pretty lace bra. Only her arms were holding it against her lovely breasts. He leaned over and drifted his lips across the exposed curves and the cleft in between, darting his tongue down between them. GG was trembling and her arms loosened, letting the wispy lace slide down a little more. Her husband's mouth followed it, working his way to the rosy tips she was vainly trying to cover. When he triumphantly closed his mouth over one swollen, sweet peak, GG arched her back and abandoned the bra, letting it flutter to the floor. She moaned helplessly as Leo's tongue played, sending electrifying sensations skittering down her spine.

Leo took his time, lazily feasting on her swollen breasts and trailing little lines of burning kisses up and down the silky smooth skin of her torso and up her throat to her ear. Delightful waves of shudders rolled down her spine and left her covered with gooseflesh. Leo's mouth drifted gradually down to her belly and he gave her a little nip just under her lowest rib. When he undid her jeans and pulled them down over her hips, she realized that she was already wet and more than ready for him. He dropped her jeans to the floor and then stood, watching her as he undressed. GG lay on the bed in only her panties, squirming a little under his eyes, unable to hold still with the way her every nerve was on fire with need.

"Leo, please," she murmured.

"Please what, baby?"

"Please, I need you. I need you closer; I need you in me."

"Oh, baby, do you have any idea how much I love you?"

"Yes." She actually gave him a satisfied, feline little smile.

With a shake of his head, he lowered his head to her thighs and kissed the sweetly sensitive spot at the top of her thigh. His mouth burned through the thin lace of her panties and made her gasp with shock. He teased her, kissing the mound between her legs, the hollow at the top of her thigh, but refusing to pull her panties off. GG was panting with desire, bucking against his mouth and he finally relented and knelt to pull the offending garment out of the way. He feasted his eyes on her naked loveliness and knew he would never, ever get tired of looking at her.

"Leo," she whispered and held up her arms for him. "Please come to me."

With a little half-growl, half-moan, he joined her on the bed. His kiss was deep and rough this time, and when his hands roamed her body, she moaned with satisfaction. He wasn't sure how she pulled it off, but suddenly he was on his back and she was straddling him. His rock-hard manhood was trapped between them and she reached down and stroked him, wringing a moan out of him when her fingers wrapped around him. She raised up a little and dragged herself up the length of him, her wet center against him until she reached the point where she could take him into her. She went slowly, inching down over him until she had taken all of him deep inside her. GG's smile was triumphant as she rose slowly and then sank down on him again. She rode him, slowly at first, and then faster and harder.

Leo was lost; lost completely in the sensation of his wife making love to him. Their tempo quickened and quickened until he couldn't bear it any longer. He flipped her over onto her back and drove into her as she wrapped her legs around him and rose to meet him.

GG felt like she was being driven into the heavens, waves of pleasure sweeping her higher and higher until she was crying out with each thrust. The room seemed to swirl with light and stars at the same time, and they exploded together in an exquisite climax, driven to the peak of sensation and rocked with shudders as they slowly came down. They clung together, quivering with little aftershocks of satisfied pleasure. It took a long time for their breathing to slow to normal and they cuddled together, so close that they were nearly one person.

"Leo," GG murmured finally, "I love you. I love you with all my heart."

Though it seemed impossible, he pulled her even closer. "My heart is yours, love. How did I ever get so lucky?"

"How did *we* ever get so lucky?" GG was nearly purring with satisfaction.

They cuddled together on the bed for a long time, moving only to pull a blanket over them when they grew too cool. They talked softly while they snuggled, talked about Leo's job possibilities, GG's letter writing to the VA patients, the home of their own they eventually wanted to buy, their plans for the future. Finally, they pulled on their bathrobes and went to the kitchen to polish off the rest of GG's cake, washed down with cold glasses of milk. When they went back to bed, they cuddled under the covers, naked, and fell asleep in each other's arms.

Chapter 2

Monday morning started out with a bang. The alarm didn't go off, and Leo leaped out of bed, fifteen minutes later than usual. GG sat up, alarmed and confused, as she heard him rushing to the bathroom, knocking over the small chair that sat in the bedroom on his way. Her eyes widened when she got a good look at the clock, and she pulled on her bathrobe and hurried to the kitchen to start a pot of coffee. By the time Leo was out of the shower and dressed, they had pretty much caught up, but the feeling of needing to hurry stuck with them. GG set a bowl of steaming oatmeal on the table along with a little plateful of toast and Leo grabbed a cup of coffee to wash down his breakfast. GG poured him a glass of juice and delivered it to him along with a kiss.

"Good morning," she said with a grin.

"Morning, baby," her husband said around a mouthful of toast. "What a way to start off the week."

"What can I do to help? I'll get your briefcase. Is your resume in it?"

Leo nodded. "I put everything in it yesterday, thank God. I hate running late."

"You're not late now; you're good. Eat your breakfast. I'll have your lunch packed in a minute." She finished making him a fat ham sandwich wrapped in waxed paper and put it into his lunchbox along with a shiny apple and a small bowl of potato salad. She knew he would put the lunchbox into the refrigerator once he got to work, so she packed his lunch every day and they added the money he would have spent buying lunch to the jar they kept to stash away money for the house. "Are you nervous about your job interview?"

Leo scraped the last bite of oatmeal out of the bowl and swallowed before he answered. "No, I'm really looking forward to it. I feel good about it. I haven't had this feeling about any of the other jobs I looked at."

GG gave him a beaming smile and said, "I'll be thinking about it all day long and sending good wishes."

"Then I have an extra good feeling about it." Leo put his breakfast dishes in the sink and kissed his wife before he left the house to start his day.

GG sat down to have her own breakfast and tidied up the kitchen before she went to the shower. By midmorning, the kitchen was clean, the bed made, floors swept, and the bathroom restored to its normal clean state. GG made her grocery list after she looked at the meals she planned to make for the week. She had learned quickly that she saved a lot of money on groceries if she planned her meals and stuck to her plan. She pulled her coat on and cast a final look around the house to see if she'd missed anything. Ten minutes later, she was pulling into the parking lot at Vance's grocery store.

"Hi, Mr. Vance," GG called as she pulled a grocery cart free.

"Hi, GG. Whoa, I mean, good morning, Mrs. Beauchamp."

GG giggled. "I love hearing that."

"How's married life?"

"Better every day," the new bride declared.

"So, are you planning to cook the Thanksgiving turkey this year?"

GG shook her head vehemently. "No, I'm definitely not ready for that yet. But I did make an applesauce stack cake for dinner yesterday and it turned out great!"

Mr. Vance was impressed. "That's not the easiest cake to make."

"Mom told me exactly how to do it. Well, I'll get out of your hair. You have a nice day."

"You too, GG."

GG started down the aisles, checking off the items on her list as she went. She checked the time; she wanted to get home in time to put together the stew and get it in the oven before Katie got there to write letters. An hour later, she slid the Dutch oven into the oven, closed the door, and set the timer. She had just enough time to stir up a pitcher full of Kool-Aid before Katie rang the doorbell. She pulled off her apron on the way to the door.

Katie was full of smiles when GG opened the door and welcomed her in. They exchanged hugs and Katie hung her coat on the coatrack beside the front door. It was bright outside but cold; winter was on its way. GG set a plate of cookies on the table and poured them each a glass of Kool-Aid and the two of them sat down with all their writing materials in front of them.

"Did you get a letter back from Boogie?" GG asked.

"Yes, they're fitting his prosthetic legs any day now. He's making jokes about it, as usual, but I know he's excited. Here's his letter; you can read it before you write back to him." The two of them took turns writing to the guys at the VA, and

Mac, the sergeant who worked there, had told them more than once how much it meant to the boys.

GG read the letter, giggling more than once. "He says once he can run the 440, he's coming to visit Boone; he's heard so much about it, he can't resist."

Katie said, "It wouldn't surprise me if he pulled that off. If anybody can do it, he can. He's been playing basketball in his wheelchair."

"They're going to miss him when he leaves the VA. He's so good at getting the other guys motivated."

"Yeah, maybe they'll have a way to keep him there, working. There are a couple of other guys doing that," Katie said.

"If he wants to, he'd be good at it. But maybe he just wants to finally get away from there," GG reflected.

"I don't know; ask him. He doesn't mind talking about pretty much anything."

"I will." The girls bent their heads over the letters and were soon writing busily. It was a good hour and a half before GG stopped and stretched. "I think I'm finished."

Katie wrote a few more sentences and then folded her letter and slid it into an envelope. "I am too. It always feels so good to address these and put them in the mail." She added her stack to GG's and grinned.

"How's Tommy doing?" GG asked.

"He's okay," Katie said thoughtfully. "He's restless. I don't think he's really happy, working as an electrician. He's not having any trouble learning the trade and he knows he can make a good living at it, but it's not making him happy."

"Has he ever talked about the war?"

"No, he doesn't want anything to do with discussing that. He gets even quieter than usual when news comes on about it and he absolutely hates seeing protests. The one thing he said about it was that those people who protest aren't protesting the war, they're protesting our boys. He said when guys get off the plane, coming home from war, they're met by a bunch of people screaming and throwing things at them. That's just so wrong!"

"So what do you think he really wants to do if it's not being an electrician?" GG asked.

"I don't know. I'm not sure he knows. I'm going to try to talk to him about it this weekend. And another thing, I don't think business college is going to be the right thing for me." Katie looked pensive.

GG sat back and stared at her. "So what do you want to do?"

"I've been thinking about it a lot, for a long time. I want to do something meaningful and I don't think being a secretary will cut it. You're the first person I've told, but I really want to be a nurse."

GG sat quiet for a few seconds and then she gave Katie a big smile. "Katie, I can totally picture you doing that. You'd make a great nurse; you have that quality that makes you seem like someone who takes care of people."

"You really think so?"

GG nodded. "Yes, I think it would suit you perfectly. You should do it!"

"It's going to be hard, but I think I can do it. My mom isn't going to like it. She just wants to see me get through this eigh-teen-month course and get a job."

GG leaned forward and said earnestly, "I know how your mom is, but once she sees you actually becoming a nurse, she's going to be proud of you. I saw her face when you walked across the stage and got your diploma. She was as proud as any mom could be."

Katie had tears in her eyes. "You really saw that?"

"I sure did. It's the most I've ever liked her. Oops... well, you know what I mean."

Katie laughed. "I know. She's not the most welcoming

person you could be around. It was just hard, what happened. She's had a hard time getting past it. And sometimes I think she's sorry about the way she handled it."

GG's face hardened. "Well, she should be. But that's all in the past now."

Katie looked down and said quietly, "It's not ever really in the past. It's always with me."

"I'm sorry, Katie. Do you want to talk about it?"

"No. I'm as at peace with it as I'll ever be. But it has a lot to do with why I want to be a nurse. Someday I'll need to tell you, because someday I need to tell Tommy if we stay together, I'm going to need a practice run before I do that."

Katie's words startled a laugh out of GG. "A practice run. Okay, I never would have thought of it that way."

Katie gave her a little grin. "It doesn't help me any to mope about it. I might as well lighten it up a little. Seriously, it's part of my life and I can't change it now. I have to accept it and make something better going forward."

GG gave her a hug and said, "I don't think I could be as strong as you. Anytime you need to make that practice run, I'm here."

Katie hugged her back and then changed the subject. "Wow, something smells good. What is it?"

"It's beef stew done in the oven. My mom gave me the recipe and this is the first time I've tried it. It *does* smell good, doesn't it?"

"It sure does. Do you want me to drop these off at the post office on my way home? I've got some studying to do."

GG got up from her chair and said, "Sure, I'll do it next week."

"Okay. I'm going to get out of here. I'll talk to you soon." Katie got her coat on and gathered the stack of letters before she hugged GG again and went out the door.

GG waved as Katie backed out of the driveway and then closed the door to the chilly air, reflecting on her conversation with her friend while she picked up all the stationery supplies and put them away in a drawer. Katie had gotten pregnant and missed all of her sophomore year of high school when her mom sent her away to a home for unwed mothers. Her baby had been given up for adoption, and Katie came back to school for her junior year, having kept up with all her studies during the year she'd missed. She'd had a really rough time at school until GG and her best friend, Sharon, befriended her and shielded her from some of the nasty girls in their class. They'd ended up with a genuine friendship, and Katie had been able to walk with the rest of them to graduate with her class. And when Sharon's brother, Tommy, had come home from his tour in Vietnam, he had persistently continued to ask Katie out until she finally gave in and accepted. They'd been seeing each other ever since. They were both quiet people who were scarred by things that had happened to them, but they were comfortable together with their silence. They could have long conversations sometimes, but they were also content to just be together without the need for talk. GG had to tease them about it sometimes.

The sound of the front door opening made GG smile and then she heard Leo call, "Hey! Where's my woman?"

"Right here!" GG was giggling as she leaped into his arms and he swung her around as he kissed her. "I guess you had a good day, huh?" She was breathless from the kiss.

"I sure did. The morning started out crazy, waking up late, but the rest of the day just got better and better."

"What happened?"

Leo nuzzled her neck and she clung to him as he walked with her to the kitchen. "What are you cooking? Whatever it is, it smells great. I could use a beer, baby."

"Okay, but what happened? It must have been something good if it put you in this mood."

Leo hadn't put her down yet, and he carried her along to the refrigerator while he got himself a beer. "You haven't told me what smells so good. Your husband is starving, you know."

"It's beef stew! Now, spill it! What happened?"

His mouth covered hers again, and she was gasping when he finally released her lips. "My job interview went about as well as I could possibly hope for. And it's the perfect job to start with; I really want it. I have a second interview on Thursday."

GG squealed with excitement and sealed his mouth with hers in another passionate kiss. "We have to celebrate!"

Leo winked at her. "Slow down, I don't have the job yet. And I'm not about to jinx it by celebrating too soon."

GG cast him a long look from under her eyelashes, touching her top lip with the tip of her tongue. "There's more than one kind of celebration, big boy."

Leo's brows shot up. "Is that right?"

"Mm hm. I could put on that little black nightie…"

Leo grabbed her and pulled her tight against him. His voice was hoarse when they finally separated from the kiss he laid on her. "I think that's the kind of celebration I could handle."

GG's face was flushed and she murmured, "The stew is ready. Since you're starving, how about we feed you, build up your strength for that celebration?"

He nuzzled her neck and nipped at her earlobe. "You're on. And don't plan on that nightie staying on for too long."

They never even turned on the TV after dinner that evening. By the middle of the following week, Leo had his first engineering job. That weekend, they splurged and went out for a steak dinner with Jack Medford and Sharon Calder, who were their closest friends. And on Sunday, they went to GG's parents' house for a lasagna dinner, then stopped by Leo's parents' house for a celebratory drink. Leo's mother poured a small glass of champagne for GG and winked at her as they all toasted Leo's new job.

Leo and GG got home just before the nightly news came on, and they sat down to watch, saddened by the casualty numbers from the war. Then a report came on that made them both sit up, frozen with shock. A commune in Ohio had been raided by police, who found large amounts of drugs and women and children who had been abused, over and over, by the men who inhabited the commune.

"Leo! That's the commune we went to." GG's eyes were huge.

Leo said grimly, "It sure is. I *knew* there was something bad going on there. But this is even worse than I imagined."

They watched intently as there was footage of ambulances taking at least twenty women and children to the hospital. The men were handcuffed and hauled off to jail. There was mass confusion at the commune, which had been locked down by police. They had placed a female police officer in the commune, undercover, and made the raid as soon as they had enough to justify it.

Suddenly, GG cried out in shock, "Oh my God, that's Stevie!" The woman she saw was drawn and emaciated, her eyes dull and haunted. "What's happened to her? I can't believe this!"

Leo said, "Stevie? Is that the girl you told me about from the music festival?"

"Yes." Tears were spilling down GG's face. "She was so beautiful—and calm and peaceful."

They watched, as Stevie was put into an ambulance, and listened to the rest of the report. Leo held GG in his arms as she wept, and a few minutes later the phone rang. Leo answered it and handed it to GG. "It's Sharon," he said.

Sharon was weeping too. "Did you see the news? Did you see her?"

"Yes, she looks so awful. And they took her off in an ambulance. What did they do to her? To all of them? We should have done something. We knew something was wrong there and we just went back home and did nothing."

"I know. But I don't know what we could have done. The police were working on it for two years, they said. So they were already investigating at the time we were there."

GG said helplessly, "Maybe if we had talked to the police, they could have moved faster."

Leo interrupted her, "Now, hold on, both of you. We didn't know anything. We just had a feeling. The police can't do anything with a feeling, and we didn't see or hear anything that we could have told them as facts."

Sharon said, "I heard him. He's right; we didn't have anything to go on but our feelings."

GG said, "I guess so. I wonder what's going to happen to all those women. And children, that's even worse! We're going to have to find out how Stevie is and what's going to happen to her."

"Yes, maybe there's something we can do to help her recover. I'm going to call Jack. You talk to Leo and maybe we can make a plan to do something constructive."

"Okay, we'll talk and figure something out. Bye for now." GG hung up the phone and told Leo what Sharon had said.

"We'll do whatever we can," Leo said, kissing her on the forehead. "You can get on the phone tomorrow and find out as much as you can from the police and hospital. As soon as I get home from work, I'll call Jack and we'll try to figure out what we can do."

GG hugged him and said, "I love you. And thank you for

understanding. We only knew Stevie for a weekend, but when I asked her if we'd ever see her again, she said we would if it was meant to be. This looks like it was meant to be."

Leo gave her a gentle kiss. "Let's go to bed. I've got a feeling we're going to have a lot to do tomorrow."

Chapter 3

G G spent a frustrating morning on the phone, trying her best to get some information on what was happening with Stevie. She had no luck with the police department. Their answer was that they couldn't give out information about an active investigation. There was a similar brick wall at the hospital; unless she was an immediate family member, they couldn't give out any information about a patient. She even tried the local newspaper, who only had what had already been released by the TV news stations. When she hung up after her last phone call, her head was aching. She got a glass of water and washed down a couple of aspirin with it, at a loss as to what to do next.

GG decided to start something for supper and give her mind a break for a little while. Maybe she was trying too hard to come up with ideas. She took the stewing hen out of the refrigerator and put it in her big stockpot to make soup. After she turned it down to a gentle simmer, she decided to bake cookies. As she slid the last tray into the oven, she had a sudden thought. She hurried to the phone and stood, thinking for a minute. With a little thought, she remembered, and called information. She jotted down the phone number that she was given and hurried back to check the cookies.

Five minutes later, GG was dialing the number of the little restaurant in Ohio that she, Leo, Jack, and Sharon had eaten at after they visited the commune. She asked for Bess and was told the waitress would be in a little later. She promised to call back and hung up. GG kept busy in the kitchen until it was late enough to call again. This time the phone was answered by a familiar-sounding voice. She explained to the waitress who she was, and Bess immediately remembered the four of them.

"Sure, I remember you. You all had the fish basket, and you left me a nice, fat tip too. What can I do for you?"

GG explained about the news report they'd seen and the woman they had recognized. "I can't get the police department to tell me anything and the hospital won't either, because I'm not a family member. I was hoping that maybe you heard more about the whole thing than what they put on TV. It was just so awful to see how bad Stevie looked. She was beautiful when we met her, and she was such a peaceful person. We've got to help her if there's any possible way that we can!"

"Geez, that's awfully nice of you. Those poor girls, we always thought there were bad things going on out there, but you could never get any of them to talk about it. Let me see what I can do; I've got a few tricks up my sleeve. If you give me your number, I can call you back after I try to find out some things."

GG said, "But it's long distance. I don't want you to have to pay for a call."

Bess laughed. "Aw, don't worry about that. I'll just use the phone here at the restaurant. He'll never know the difference. He's always calling places long distance. And, besides, he owes me."

"Are you talking about your boss?" GG asked.

"Yeah. Well, he thinks so. He's the owner, but he'd never make it without me." Bess wrote down GG's phone number and promised to get back to her soon, although she cautioned GG that it would probably take a day or two.

GG thanked Bess profusely and hung up with a feeling of relief. She was sure that Bess was going to find some things out for her. She was still worried about Stevie, but now she felt like she was going to have a chance to help her. It was hard to wait for information, but she had plenty to keep her busy for the rest of the afternoon. She decided to make chicken and dumplings out of her stewed chicken, and she put a nice green salad together to go along with it. Then she put a load of clothes in the used washer they had found and turned it on. By the time Leo got home, the house was neat and clean, the laundry was folded and put away, and the kitchen was full of wonderful smells.

"Wow! It smells great in here. What are you cooking?" Leo asked, kissing his wife.

"Chicken and dumplings," GG said with a grin. "And I made cookies."

"Are you trying to make me fat?"

"No." GG laughed at him. "You work too hard to get fat. The police department and hospital wouldn't tell me anything."

"Nothing at all?"

"Nope. But then I had an idea and I called that restaurant where we ate after we went to see the commune. Remember the waitress? Her name was Bess. She seemed to know quite a bit about the commune."

"Oh, yeah, I remember her. I don't know if I would have remembered her name. Did you talk to her?"

GG nodded. "Yes, and she remembered us too. She promised to try to find out something about Stevie. She said they always thought there were bad things going on at the commune, but they couldn't ever get any of the girls to talk about it."

"Does she really think she can find something out?"

"Maybe. She said she has some tricks up her sleeve." GG smiled. "She's such a nice woman."

Leo gave her a hard hug. "That was good thinking, baby. Jack's going to call me when he gets home from class. Bess might be our best chance, though. She's right there in the community."

"Yeah, that's what I thought. And she's the kind of person people talk to, so that helps."

By the time they had talked to Jack and Sharon, they knew that all they had, at least for the time being, was Bess. With a sigh, GG realized that she just had to be patient and wait to hear from her. She and Leo enjoyed their supper and watched some TV until GG had to admit that Bess wasn't going to call that night. She had a hard time falling asleep, worrying about Stevie and hoping there would turn out to be some way they could help. She woke early in the morning, after a restless night, and worked off some nervous energy by making pancakes and sausage for Leo for breakfast. He kissed her goodbye and went off to work, after assuring GG that she would hear from Bess soon.

It was the middle of the afternoon when the phone rang, and GG rushed to answer it, to find Bess on the other end of the line.

"Hi, GG," the waitress said. "I found out some stuff. I had to pretend to be Stevie's cousin and told them all about Stevie disappearing and the family not hearing from her again, but I finally got them to talk some. She's not charged with anything because she didn't have any drugs on her. But she's definitely been using God-knows-what, and she's in really rotten physical shape. She's not talking much to them, and she's going to be in the hospital for a few days. She was really malnourished when they brought her in and she's been sexually abused and just really treated rotten. She's scared to death of everything and has terrible nightmares. Once she's ready to leave the hospital, if she doesn't let them know how to contact her family, she'll be on her own."

GG was appalled. "On her own? But she won't have anywhere to go, will she?"

"No, probably not. Which means she'll probably try to hitchhike to someplace big enough so that she can live on the streets. Or something even worse could happen to her."

GG had tears in her eyes. "I can't let that happen to her."

"The nurse I talked to said I was the closest thing to a family tie that they knew of at this point, and she promised to let me know when she's going to be released. As soon as I know, I'll call you if you want."

"Yes! Yes, please let me know. Maybe we can think of something, maybe even come and try to get her to come with us."

Bess said, "GG, you should be ready for how she's going to be. She might not even remember you, she might be hostile, she might be scared of you. She might not let you help her."

GG said, "Well, we have to try. I can't live with myself if I don't at least try."

"Okay, I'll call you as soon as I know. I hope you can help her." Bess hung up, and GG had to wipe away tears.

By the time Leo got home from work, GG had called everyone she could think of who might know something about how to help people who had ended up like Stevie. In Boone, there weren't many people who ever got into the drug culture, but she did get some bits and pieces of useful information. The pastor who had married her and Leo gave her some phone numbers of counselors and charities that worked with drug cases. There was at least one halfway house that took in women with problems like drug and alcohol abuse, not too far from Boone, and there were more resources in Indianapolis.

GG looked up from the notebook she was busily writing in and blinked in surprise. "Leo! What are you doing home already?"

Leo's eyebrows shot up. "Already? I'm almost a half hour late."

"Oh, my gosh! I completely lost track of time. I haven't even started dinner yet."

"What are you doing there? You've got pages of notes." Leo was staring down at the table.

"Oh! I have to tell you all about it. But I've got to get dinner going. I can't believe I didn't even know what time it was." GG was completely flustered.

"Baby, don't worry about dinner. We have plenty of chicken and dumplings left over, don't we?"

"Yes, but we just had that last night."

"And it was delicious last night. That doesn't bother me at all. Heck, we can have sandwiches, as far as I'm concerned. Tell me what you're doing here."

"Well, let me at least put the dumplings on to warm up before I tell you about all this."

GG bustled around the kitchen after she belatedly gave her husband a kiss, and he drank a beer after he changed out of his work clothes. Finally, she had dinner warming, and she explained all about her conversation with Bess and all the phone calls she had made that day.

"Wow," Leo said finally, "you really found out a lot of stuff today."

"So, is it all right? Can we go when they release Stevie from the hospital and help her?"

Leo felt a little warning bell in his head. "You're going to have to be careful about what you expect," he cautioned. "Stevie may not want help. And she's a grown woman. If she refuses it, there's nothing you can actually do about it. If she chooses to walk away, and you don't have any idea what's going to happen to her next, you're going to have to accept that."

GG stuck her lower lip out stubbornly. "But we have to try. Right? You're okay with that?"

"GG." Leo set his beer down and held his wife's shoulders as he looked closely into her eyes. "Yes, I'm okay with trying. But you have to be okay with the possibility of her refusing. If you can't, then we're going to have a problem over this."

"If she absolutely refuses to let us help, then I guess I'll have to accept it. But she's not going to. She's lost and she's been abused. She's going to need help. And I have to believe she's going to want it." GG was clearly going to expect the best possible outcome.

Leo sighed. "We'll try. That's all I'm promising. You should get all the information you can about those halfway houses and what it takes to get them to take her in."

"I will. I'll find out everything I can. Thank you, Leo, thank you!" GG was smiling as she whirled around to the stove to stir the dumplings.

Leo shook his head slowly. There was a strong possibility that his young wife was going to get another lesson in the realities of life. And she wasn't going to like it a bit. He would be there for her, but he knew she would take it hard if she couldn't succeed at helping Stevie. It would rip his gut out, but it was a lesson she might have to learn. So he would hope for the best and prepare for the worst.

Leo had only one week left to work at his job, and then he was going to have a week off before he started his engineering job. He'd planned to spend most of that time brushing up on the coursework he'd had in college. Some of that time would most likely be spent dealing with Stevie. That was okay; he knew he was ready for his job. He leafed through the notes GG had written out, then he sat down to take a closer look.

"GG, let's organize all this into the most likely things that work and down to the less likely, but maybe necessary. Put it into some kind of order."

"That's a good idea. It's kind of scattered; I just took separate notes from everyone I talked to."

Leo nodded. "That's okay; that's how you start out. Now we can organize it." He started reading and making notes of his own as he went through the papers. Then he started some lists. By the time they sat down to eat, it was a lot easier to look through all the things GG had found out.

"This makes a lot more sense now," GG said when she looked through it after dinner. "First things are first, and the most important things are clear. You're a lot more organized than I am."

"It's the engineering brain." Leo grinned at her. "How long did Bess say they were keeping her in the hospital?"

"She said a few days. She'll call me as soon as the nurse calls her to tell her when they expect to release her."

"Okay, good. She should be getting released while I have some days off work. I think we'd better go to visit her before she's supposed to be released. We need to get an idea of how she feels, and if she's going to accept help. You know, have some idea of what we'll be facing when she actually walks out of the hospital." Leo stacked everything in neat piles and put notes on each stack to label the contents.

GG walked over to him and curled up in his lap. "Thank you so much for this. I know it's more than most people would do, and I love you for it."

"Well, I love your big heart, so I guess I kind of have an obligation. Right?"

GG laughed. "I'll accept that."

"So you didn't even have time to make dessert?"

GG looked crestfallen. "No, I'm sorry. But we do have ice cream. Will that do?"

"Ice cream sounds fabulous. Put a cherry on top?"

GG laughed. "I don't have any cherries. I'll give you an extra scoop."

Leo buried his face in her neck, making her squeal when he nibbled at her earlobe. "An extra scoop will be perfect. And then I'll give *you* something extra."

"Ooh!" GG bounded up and went to the cupboard for bowls. "I love getting something extra! Let's have ice cream."

Leo's "something extra" took until the late night hours, and they fell asleep cuddled together and happy.

Chapter 4

Leo, GG, and Sharon were on their way to Ohio to the hospital where Stevie was a patient. They were quiet in between bursts of conversation while Leo drove. They had no idea what to expect and weren't even sure that Stevie would remember the two girls. Leo tried to prepare them for a disappointment, but GG was her usual optimistic self; Sharon was more realistic about it. GG talked to Bess again before they set out, and Bess told her that the nurse said that Stevie was much improved from when she had been brought in. But she had been traumatized, and she had a long way to go. It made GG sad and angry when she thought about the serene, joyful Stevie they had met at the music festival.

When they got to the hospital, they asked for the nurse Bess had been talking to. Bess had checked to make sure she would be working when they arrived.

"So, you're the friends Bess told me about. I'm glad you're here to at least try to help that poor girl. She's never said a word about having a family. She's met with a therapist several times and she's said a little about what happened to her, but not much. They were drugging her, keeping her under their control, but one thing she's been adamant about is that she hasn't ever taken drugs on her own. She said she used to smoke pot a little bit, but nothing else." The nurse, Nina, was disgusted by what had been done to the women at the commune. And the kids! She, personally, thought they should keep the men in jail and throw away the key.

GG asked, "Is she addicted? Is she having withdrawal? I don't know very much about all this."

"No, she was starved half to death when she got here, but they didn't drug her heavily enough or for long enough to get her addicted. That's a big plus for her. She had an infection, and the doc treated her with antibiotics, and that's much better. She has trouble keeping food down. She has to eat really small portions, so we've been offering them to her pretty much hourly. She has awful nightmares and wakes up screaming. Then she's terrified that someone is going to beat her for it. I don't know what all she went through in that place, but it must have been terrible. Her biggest problems are going to be psychological. It's going to take time for her to feel safe again."

GG was heartbroken at what she was hearing. "Is there anything more we should know before we see her?"

Nina said, "No, I think you should just be gentle and play it by ear. You and Sharon can go in and see her but she doesn't know Leo, right?"

Leo shook his head. "No, only the girls met her."

"Okay, then only the girls should talk to her for now. Come on. I'll take you to her room."

Leo gave GG a quick hug and wished her luck. Nina went first, greeting Stevie, who jumped when the nurse walked into her room. Her eyes were wide and wary, and she huddled under the blanket on the bed. GG and Sharon were shocked at the sight of her. She was thin to the point of emaciation, and her once beautiful hair was dull and threaded with gray.

"Stevie, some friends of yours are here to see you."

Stevie looked panicked and said, "That's not possible."

Nina opened the curtains to let the outside light in. "Why not, sweetie?"

"Because I don't have any friends," Stevie said simply.

GG took a step closer. "I know you might not remember us, but we met you at a music festival. We stayed on the hill with you for that weekend. We had a lot of fun."

Stevie stared at her for a long minute and finally said, "You're from Indiana."

GG smiled and said, "That's right. I'm GG and this is Sharon. We'd never been to a music festival before, and we had a great time."

Stevie's eyes filled with tears and she said, "That was before. Before all the bad stuff."

GG and Sharon moved closer and GG said, "It was a magical weekend; the music was so amazing."

"That was the good time. I should have gone where the sun was warm and the water was blue. That's what I was supposed to do." Stevie's eyes were far away.

"I remember," Sharon said softly. "You said you wanted to grow vegetables and weave cloth and be where the sun shone all the time."

"I never got there."

GG sat down in the chair beside the bed and said, "We want to help you if we can, Stevie."

Stevie looked at her curiously. "Why?"

GG smiled at her. "Because you helped us."

"I did?"

"Yes, you sure did. We were so far out of our league when we got to that music festival, and you just kind of tucked us under your wing and took care of us. We had a wonderful weekend, and we've never forgotten you."

A tear spilled over and ran slowly down Stevie's cheek. "That was when I could help people. I didn't know there were such awful people out there. It was supposed to be a safe place, but it wasn't. It was all a lie. They even hurt the little ones." Her voice broke and tears coursed down her face. "How could anybody do that?"

GG's heart broke for her. "I don't know. I do know they're in jail now, and they're not going to let them out. And you're safe now."

"But they're not going to let me stay here. I have to leave. Then it won't be safe."

Sharon said, "That's why we're here. We want to help you go to a safe place when you leave here. We want you to feel safe forever."

"Is there a place like that?" Stevie's voice was weary and hopeless.

"Yes," GG said firmly. "We're not going to let you go to a place that isn't like that."

Stevie gazed at the two of them for a long time. "Maybe I do have some friends." She closed her eyes, leaning back against the pillows.

"We'll come back a little later," Nina said. "You rest now."

They left the room quietly, and GG and Sharon had to stop and hug each other hard.

Nina said, "It's good that you're here. I'd hate to see her just walk out of here on her own."

GG said fiercely, "That's not happening. She's going some-place safe if I have to take her to my own home. She was so beautiful and carefree when we met her. She's obviously seen things that *nobody* should ever see."

Nina said briskly, "I think I should take you to see the social services administrator here at the hospital. I know you did a lot of research on possible places where Stevie could go, and she's the person who could help guide you to the right one."

They had joined Leo in the waiting area and he said, "That sounds like a good idea. Let's do it."

Nina led them through the halls to another waiting area, where she had them take seats while she arranged the meeting. She was back in a few minutes. "Joyce can see you in an hour. She has a meeting in a few minutes that she has to keep. There's a coffee shop across the street, and our cafeteria here is pretty good if you want to go downstairs."

"Let's do that," Leo said. "My stomach is growling."

"Okay, take the elevator to the lobby level, and there are signs to direct you to the cafeteria. You'll be meeting with Joyce Fisher, in the social services office, right back here."

"Thank you, Nina," GG said.

"Thank you. You're giving that girl a chance."

The girls filled Leo in on the conversation they'd had with Stevie while they all had a light lunch. They were back in the waiting area ten minutes early for their meeting with the social service administrator. GG had her thick folder full of information she had gathered over the last few days. A few minutes later, the office door opened and a forty-something woman stepped out to greet them. They all introduced themselves and took seats in the administrator's office. She put them at ease right away.

"All right, call me Joyce, and I'll call all of you by your first names if that's all right." At their nods, she went on. "I understand you're here because you want to look out for the welfare of Stevie Wright. Are you family?"

"No," Leo said. "My wife, GG, and her friend, Sharon, met Stevie at a music festival. They'd never been to anything like that before, and Stevie looked out for them for the weekend. They all had a good time, no bad experiences, and they never forgot Stevie."

Joyce looked at the girls curiously. "What was Stevie like then?"

GG said, "She was beautiful and exotic. She was really peaceful and calm, and she just wanted to live a life of peace and love. She was hoping to go to a commune in a place with beaches, water, and sunshine. She was just a happy, gentle soul, but she knew her way around."

Sharon said, "It was like she was really intelligent, but she just wanted the whole world to be loving and peaceful."

Joyce had a stack of paperwork of her own in front of her. "Well, she went to a commune, all right, but it wasn't sunshine and blue water. That place was a hellhole. Stevie is actually in better condition than most of the others. She hadn't been there as long as the rest of them. She's not addicted, which is the best thing about all this. But I think it crushed her to see what those bastards did to the kids. That's the root of her trauma, and it's going to be hard for her to get over it, as much as she can."

GG and Sharon looked horrified. "Those poor babies!" GG said.

"So Stevie is going to need therapy and a safe place where she won't be getting hit with any surprises. She needs a routine that she can count on. Let's take a look at that paperwork you brought."

Joyce went through the notes, sometimes comparing GG's notes with her own paperwork. She crossed out several of the places GG had come up with, and put stars on a couple of them. Then she sat back and said, "Okay, let's go through this. You did a good job, GG, of finding these resources. Some of these places are not doing the work that they claim to be doing. They collect funds from the government and do very little to help the people who live in these so-called halfway houses and shelters. But three of these are good places. They would be the kind of shelter that Stevie needs, and she would get the therapy that she needs, too."

"How would we go about getting her into one of these places?" Leo asked.

"Well, first, let's look at them more closely. Do you know anything about Stevie's family?"

GG and Sharon both said no.

"That means we don't know where they might be. So two of these are here in Ohio, and one is actually in Indianapolis. How involved do you want to be? Are you just looking to get her into a safe place and that would be the extent of things for you? That's certainly more than your share of looking out for her. You barely know her."

GG and Sharon both looked blank. GG said, "I guess we didn't think any further than to make sure that she doesn't just get turned out into the streets. We're not in any position to be responsible for her, but we wanted to help her."

Joyce gave them a smile. "She's lucky to have met you, crossed paths with you. I'll be offering to help all of the women who were brought here to get help from a place like these, but very few, if any, of them, will take me up on it. They'll go off on their own on the streets, and come to even more harm than they have already. Some of them will try to go back to the commune."

GG and Sharon looked horrified.

"They will. Of course, the police have shut that place down. And then, they'll just be wandering around, looking for a place to eat and sleep. The children will go to Children's Services. If their mothers want to get them back, they'll have to prove themselves to be fit parents. That's going to be next to impossible, considering their circumstances. Most of the children will end up in foster care, and the mothers will end up in the streets, prostituting and doing drugs. My point is, if you three get Stevie into a safe home where she has a chance of starting over, you'll have done her an amazing favor."

GG said thoughtfully, "Well, we can't be responsible for

her, but I would like to stay in touch with her, maybe visit her when I can, see how she's doing. I don't want to just drop her off someplace and then walk away and forget her."

Sharon nodded in agreement. "Yeah, I feel the same way."

"Okay. Well, then let's look first at the shelter in Indianapolis. You'd be a lot closer to her there than either of the places here in Ohio."

They combed through the paperwork, and Joyce made a call to the shelter to see if they had an opening. When they did, they agreed to fax paperwork to the hospital to be filled out and faxed back to them. They spent a good hour with the administrator, and she finally sat back and said, "Well, we've put it in motion. They'll have an approval for us, if they grant it, by sometime tomorrow morning. Then we have to convince Stevie to go. She's going to be scared. That's when your support is going to be important to her. Once she gets there, they'll help her. It's a good place. I had a niece of my own who went there for help. Today, she's a kindergarten teacher and she's well and happy."

"That's wonderful," Sharon said with a smile.

"When do you think they're going to release Stevie from the hospital?" Leo asked.

"Honestly, she could go now. But they'll hold off until we have an answer from the shelter, and give us some time to get her to agree to go."

"We need to find a place to spend the night," Leo said. "It's too far to drive back home now and come right back tomorrow."

Joyce held up a finger and picked up the phone again. In a couple of minutes, she had rooms arranged for them at The Inn downtown. "The Inn is nice, it's spotlessly clean, and they'll give you a very low rate because the hospital is sending you there. They have a great dining room, too."

The three of them thanked Joyce for all her help and

stopped to see Stevie again before they left the hospital. By the time they checked into The Inn, they were all mentally worn out. They had brought overnight bags, knowing that if they were able to do anything, they were going to have to spend the night, and by the time they had dinner, they were ready to retire to their clean, comfortable rooms.

Chapter 5

The group from Boone was back in Joyce's office at 9 am, coffee in hand. They sat around the small conference table that was off to the side, so she could be near her phone. She hadn't gotten an approval yet from the shelter, but she expected it soon. She had paperwork, for them all to look at, that told them more about the shelter itself.

"There are only women at this shelter," Joyce said. "No men live there and no children do, either. Both of those factors are good for Stevie. She's not going to be able to be around men for some time, the therapist believes, and to be around children would just be too hard for her, given what she saw in the commune. Most of the women there have been abused. The atmosphere is quiet and protective. They'll give her a couple of days to settle in and get to know her way around. Then she'll be expected to do certain chores there, to help pay for her stay, and she will be expected to attend therapy. There is a library and activity room there where the ladies can read, write, work at crafts in their free time. Eventually, as she improves enough, they'll give her the opportunity to work outside the shelter and part of her pay will go to the shelter.

They have relationships with a number of employers who can accommodate special needs for their employees. They'll do their very best to try to put her in a place where she can work but still feel secure and comfortable. It's always hard at first, but it's something they have to do."

GG was looking at pictures of the interior of the shelter. "It looks nice, not fancy, but clean and comfortable. Is it a big, old house?"

"It is. It was once a private residence and the owner willed it to the shelter, which was, at the time, in a building that wasn't nearly as nice. The benefactor also provided a chunk of money to have it converted into what you see here. The shelter runs on private donations and the money they take in, which is not much. There's a fundraiser or two every year that usually helps a lot. When you go back home, I'll give you some flyers that describe the work they do and give information on how to donate. If you'll pass it around, they might pick up a good donor or two."

"Of course," Leo said, "I'm starting a new job at an engineering firm. Once I get to know people, I'll make sure to pass them around."

Sharon offered, "And I'm pre-law at IU. I'll do the same. And Jack, my boyfriend is pre-med; I'm sure he'll do the same."

GG said, "My life is right in Boone, but I'll do what I can. Leo, your dad has a lot of connections; would he help?"

Leo smiled. "You know he will."

They all went over the paperwork and talked about how to approach Stevie until Joyce's phone rang. The first call was about something else, as was the second. But, the third time the phone rang, it was the approval Joyce was hoping for. They promised to fax the necessary paperwork over and just asked them to let them know when they were on their way. All of them sat back in relief when Joyce relayed the news to them. In a few minutes, she had the paperwork and they got ready to see Stevie.

"I still think only the girls should go in. Once she agrees, we'll have to introduce her to you, Leo, since you'll be driving her there."

GG and Sharon looked at each other. Sharon said, "We'll sit in back and put Stevie between us. We'll do all we can to keep her from being scared."

Joyce said, "We had quite a lot of clothing donated from people around here after all this happened. After we talk to her, her therapist will want some time with her. If you two would help pick out a few outfits for her, that would help."

GG said immediately, "Absolutely. That's no trouble at all. Do you think we should buy her some things?"

Joyce said, "We can see what is in the donations. The shelter has an excellent supply of personal hygiene products, so we don't have to worry about that. But we may need some underthings and socks. Hopefully there are some shoes in the donations."

GG said earnestly, "We'll get whatever she needs. Right, Leo?"

Leo nodded without hesitation. "Yes, no worries."

A few minutes later, GG and Sharon were walking into Stevie's room, Joyce along with them, with a small stack of paperwork. Stevie looked a little better; she had some of her color back and had had a shower after breakfast. She looked up warily, but when she saw it was GG and Sharon, she relaxed and even gave them a small smile.

The three of them sat around her bed and GG said, "Good morning! You look better this morning. How was your night?"

Stevie picked at the blanket and finally said, "It was restless, but I think I only had two nightmares. I got some sleep."

Sharon reached for her hand and Stevie's eyes widened in

alarm, but after a slight hesitation, she let Sharon take her hand. Sharon said, "That's good; I'm glad you did."

Joyce said, "Stevie, we've done all we can for you here in the hospital. Your friends have been helping me look for a safe place for you to go, and we think we've found one. May I show you some pictures and tell you about it?"

Stevie's eyes were wide now and she began to tremble. But she said faintly, "Okay."

Joyce took her time, showing Stevie the pictures and describing the shelter to her. Stevie was visibly relieved to hear that there would be no men there. She was sad at the thought of no children, but GG could see that she was relieved about it, too. Joyce was firm but gentle as she made sure that Stevie understood what her choices were. Basically, to hit the streets on her own or to go to the shelter and get a second chance.

Stevie looked at GG and Sharon and asked, "You'll take me there?"

Both girls nodded immediately and GG said, "My husband is going to be driving us but we'll be with you all the way."

Stevie sat silently for a long minute and then said, "I have to try it. I can't go out there by myself; I know I can't. I had a chance once to get away from the commune and I was too afraid of being by myself to do it. I'll go; I have to."

Sharon said, "You're making a smart decision, Stevie. You're going to get your life back."

Joyce said, "Sharon's right, Stevie, you have a chance now. I'm going to take care of all the details and we'll get you ready to go."

In less than an hour, they were ready to leave. GG and Sharon carefully introduced Leo to Stevie and, though she avoided eye contact with him, she didn't panic. When they arrived at the address they were looking for, she began to tremble and gripped GG's hand hard.

"It's okay, Stevie, you're going to be safe here," Sharon said.

Leo waited outside as the three women went to the door of the big house. There was a wide front porch, with a swing at one end. It was surrounded by a large yard with big, old shade trees. There was nothing threatening about it and even though Stevie was visibly nervous, she walked forward with them without protest. A pleasant-looking woman answered the door and welcomed them with a warm smile. The paperwork took only a minute, since most of it had been done already by Joyce, and the woman, whose name was Lila, showed them around the shelter. She explained their routine to Stevie as they walked around the place, showing her the activities room and the kitchen, dining room and big laundry room. She showed Stevie to the room that would be hers and explained that there was one bathroom for each three residents' rooms. Stevie's room was furnished with a bed, a dresser, a nightstand with a lamp, a comfortable chair, and there was a small closet.

Stevie's eyes were huge. "This room is just for me?"

Lila smiled at her. "Yes, this is your space. You're responsible for keeping it clean and you have to take your turn at cleaning your bathroom, too. You'll have other duties, but not today or tomorrow. We want you to get settled in and comfortable with your surroundings. There are snacks and drinks in the kitchen that you can help yourself to. Everybody takes a turn cooking meals. There are therapy sessions for you and group sessions too. I know they'll make you nervous at first, but you'll get used to them and they'll really help you a lot. That's what we want more than anything, to see you heal and get strong. The things that happened to you weren't your fault and we want you to feel that right to the bottom of your soul."

Stevie was nearly overcome with emotion at her words and Lila briskly went on to something else. "You can put your bag here in your closet and unpack your things later; I have a little more to show you and then you can have some privacy." She took Stevie to a room that was piled and hung with clothing, personal items, and shoes. "We get a lot of donations and you can find things in here that will fit you. Find and take what you need and just leave these little stickers that are on everything on this clipboard by the door. That's how we kind of keep track of what we have and what we need."

Stevie looked stunned. "Really?"

"Yes. Don't take what you don't need, but don't hesitate to take what you do. It's kind of a weird system, but it seems to work for us. Why don't you come back to the kitchen for a minute and get yourself a snack and a drink to tide you over until dinner? You look like you're getting very tired and your friends will need to get on their way soon."

Stevie looked a little panicked at the idea of GG and Sharon leaving, but she was so overwhelmed that she took it pretty well. At Lila's urging, she selected a crisp, red apple and a little package of peanut butter crackers along with a small carton of milk. GG and Sharon said their goodbyes without drawing them out, heeding what Joyce had told them, and in a couple of minutes, they were back in the car. Both of them shed some tears as they drove away, but Leo was quick to tell them what a good thing they had done.

"It was just so hard to walk away from her," GG said, wiping away tears.

"Just take a second to think of where she'd be right now if you hadn't done this," Leo responded. "You two may very well have just saved her life."

The girls looked at each other and gave each other a watery nod. "She's safe," Sharon said.

"She is. Leo, we couldn't have done this without you," GG said. "Thank you for helping us; you never hesitated."

Thankfully, the mood lightened. They drove for about a

half hour and GG suddenly said, "I don't know about you guys, but I am so starved! Can we stop for something?"

"Hallelujah!" Leo exclaimed. "I'm so hungry, I figured you all could hear my stomach growling!" He pulled into the first diner he saw and they piled out of the car.

Over giant, juicy burgers and piles of fries, they talked happily about the way the whole thing had gone. Leo ordered a second burger and the girls laughed at him while they ate hot fudge sundaes. It was a happy, satisfied ride home and they already had plans to visit Stevie in about a month, after she'd had time to adjust to her new life. It was dark when they drove back into Boone, and they were all exhausted. Leo dropped Sharon off, and they exchanged their goodnight hugs and went their separate ways.

Lying in bed, GG and Leo talked about the day until Leo realized that GG had stopped answering him. With a little chuckle, he kissed her forehead and tucked the blankets a little higher under her chin before he heaved a sigh and dropped off to sleep.

GG woke first in the morning and stretched like a sleepy kitten before the events of the previous day popped into her head. She felt a little pang whenever she pictured Stevie's face when they had left; she'd looked scared and lost. GG firmly reminded herself that her friend was in a safe place where she would be protected, and she wondered if she was feeling more secure yet. Lila had told them to feel free to call to check on how things were going, but she'd also told them to give it a few days. Stevie would need time to adjust. She was going to have to keep very busy so she could resist the temptation to call.

A few days later, GG called to check on her friend. She spoke to Lila, who told her that things were going as well as she had hoped. Stevie was still having nightmares and she was reluctant to speak when she was in group therapy sessions, but she had just begun, the day before, to open up a little in her private therapy session. She was completely cooperative about doing her part with chores in the house and she was spending some time drawing when she had free time. Lila suggested that GG give her another week and, if things were still progressing, Lila would call Stevie to the phone the next time they spoke. GG felt better after she hung up the phone and she smiled through the rest of her day, cleaning and cooking with the most energy she'd had since they had left Stevie at the shelter. Sharon was thrilled with the news when GG called her after her classes were over for the day and she promised to tell Jack all about it.

GG spent the rest of the afternoon making Leo's favorite meal, meatloaf, baked potatoes, and peas with tiny, little onions and her homemade peach crisp for dessert. When he got home after work, he knew immediately what they were having.

"Wow! It smells amazing in here. What are we celebrating?"

GG brought him a beer and sat in his lap to tell him all about her conversation with Lila. He hugged her tight, loving seeing her so happy. "And next week, I can call again, and if things are still going well, I get to talk to Stevie!"

"I'm happy for her," Leo said. "She could be wandering the streets with no place to go if it weren't for you."

"If it weren't for all of us," GG corrected him.

"Yes, but you were the one who made sure that all of us did everything we could. You were the one who thought of calling Bess. You didn't give up until you found a way to help. That's more special than you know, baby."

"I just wanted her to have a chance to be safe," GG said simply.

Leo kissed her, long and hard. "No wonder I fell in love with you."

GG nestled her head on his shoulder and said, "I didn't even ask you how your day was."

"It was good. I'm going to be working on a project with Mike starting next week. I'll be doing more learning than anything, but I'll get to contribute too. It's pretty exciting."

"What kind of project is it?"

"It's a reroute of a road for the purpose of putting in a new bridge. The plans for the bridge are already done, but the road has to be widened to accommodate the increase in traffic at this site and the bridge will be four lane instead of two. If things go well, I'll be in on the next bridge project from the beginning. How well I do with this will make the difference."

GG hugged him tight and said, "You're going to be amazing. I just know it."

"I know I'm going to work my hardest and do my best."

"Are you hungry?"

"I'm starving! I'd like to go change clothes. Do I have time?"

GG checked the clock and nodded. "Yep. Dinner will be ready in about fifteen minutes."

It was a perfect evening for the young married couple.

Chapter 6

Boone seemed to be bustling with activities over the next few months. Katie started nursing school, taking extra classes to make up for lost time. Tommy finished his apprenticeship and got his electrician's license. Sharon and Jack were both working hard toward their undergraduate degrees. Jack was a year ahead of Sharon, but she was taking extra classes in hopes of catching up. Stevie was beginning to come out of her shell and talked on the phone to GG regularly. GG was finding that most of the letter writing to the VA was falling on her shoulders, since Sharon and Katie were so busy with school. She didn't mind, but it was a little lonely. It seemed that all of her friends were busy pursuing meaningful careers and she began to feel a little left out of life. Even her husband was often preoccupied with his new career. She was truly happy for them all, but GG was at loose ends once again, trying to figure out how she was going to make a difference to people.

It was the middle of the morning and GG was standing in the middle of her spotlessly clean house, hands on hips, staring around her little domain. The laundry was finished, the house was clean, the refrigerator was shining from the deep cleaning she had done on it the day before. Even the oven was freshly cleaned. She wondered idly if she should strip the bed and wash the sheets but realized she had just done it three days earlier. She had sent out a stack of letters to the VA the day before and she literally didn't know what to do with the rest of her day. She called her mother, but she was on her way out the door to have lunch with friends and the call was over in a flash. Leo's parents and sisters were visiting relatives in New York and wouldn't be back for another week. By the time Leo got home from work, GG was feeling incredibly sorry for herself.

"Hi, baby, how was your day?" He came through the door in his usual good mood, satisfied with the day he'd had at work and happy to be home with his loving wife.

"Oh, my day was just lovely. How was yours?"

Completely missing the warning signs, Leo said, "It was great. I made some changes to our plans and after Mike looked them over, he gave full approval and commended me for seeing the need to make the changes. Looks like I'm going to be working on that next project, like I hoped."

GG rolled her eyes. "That's great. I'm going to check on dinner."

Leo watched her walk away, finally getting the negative vibes from her and wondering just what was going on with her. He followed her into the kitchen and got himself a beer. "So what did you do today?"

GG banged the lid down on the stewpot and said, "I did the same things I do every day. Make the bed, do the laundry, clean the house, cook dinner."

Her husband set his beer down and put his arms around her, nuzzling her neck. "And you do a wonderful job of it. It's good to come home to; you're making this little house a real home."

50

Irritated, she shrugged away from him and started getting dishes out of the cupboard. "Oh, just the way your mother's book said I should?"

Leo laughed. "Right. That book made its way to the trash a long time ago, didn't it?"

GG said tartly, "Well, sounds like I'm doing a bang-up job of following its instructions."

"Did something happen today?"

"No, Leo, nothing happened today. Just like every day. The house was clean and laundry all done at ten this morning. So I had the entire rest of the day with basically nothing to do."

"Good, you had some spare time." Leo missed her point completely.

GG whirled around and said, "Is that supposed to be funny?"

Her husband looked perplexed. "No, not at all. Why should you have to spend all your time working? You should have time to do something for yourself, something you enjoy."

"Like what, Leo? My whole life is right here. I'm the devoted housewife your mother wanted me to be. What else am I supposed to do?"

Leo was beginning to lose patience. "Take up a hobby. Go to the library and find a good book. Take a class, something you've always wanted to do. You can do anything you want to."

"Go change clothes. Dinner will be ready as soon as the bread is done." GG turned back to setting the table.

Leo stared at her for another moment and then decided to give her a minute to cool off. He went to the bedroom and changed out of his work clothes, returning to the kitchen just as his wife took the bread out of the oven. "What's for dinner, baby? It smells delicious."

"Beef stew and fresh bread," GG said shortly.

"Sounds great. Can I help you with anything?"

"No. It's all ready." She set a big serving bowl of stew on the hot pad she had placed on the table and then set a plate of freshly sliced, warm bread on there as well. She bowed her head while Leo said a quick prayer and then ladled stew into their bowls. Leo passed the bread to her and she took it without a word.

"This is really good," Leo said. "Did you talk to Stevie today?"

"No. I talk to Stevie on Thursdays."

"Oh, that's right. What's everyone else up to?"

"I have no idea what anyone else is up to. They're all busy; they have school and work and no time to waste. Even my mother is too busy for wasting time." GG's answer was clipped.

Leo set his spoon down and looked at her with a frown. "What exactly do you mean by wasting time?"

"They have things to do. They don't have time to spend talking to me, just because I don't have anything to do."

Once again, Leo was losing patience. "Then maybe you should get something to do, besides sit here feeling sorry for yourself."

GG's cheeks turned pink and she gave a little gasp of outrage. "Feeling sorry for myself? That's what you think I'm doing?"

"Well, what would you call it? You're a perfectly intelligent woman, GG. There's no reason for you to just hang around the house waiting for something to come to you. You want things to do? Start a hobby. Take a class. Volunteer someplace. It's not that hard."

"Well, that's easy for you to say, isn't it? You've got a brand new career that you have to put lots of time and attention into. You're doing something you love every day, something fulfilling. You don't have to go out looking for some way to spend your time. You have a-a *purpose!*" GG was angry.

"Are you seriously going to sit here and have a temper tantrum because you're bored?" Leo's patience was officially gone.

"I'm not having a damn temper tantrum!" GG shouted.

Leo rose from his chair and GG suddenly realized that she had gone too far. Jumping up, she fled from the kitchen and locked herself in the bathroom. She heard her husband come to the door and unsuccessfully try to open the door. "GG Beauchamp, you unlock this door and get your pretty little butt out here."

"No! Go away and leave me alone." Her voice wavered a little.

"Don't make me force this door open," Leo warned her.

"I'm not coming out." She heard him walk away and then return a minute later. Then she heard a metallic rattle at the door and a few seconds later, it opened. "Leo, you leave me alone."

"GG, do you remember that long talk we had before we got married? The one about the ground rules of our marriage?"

"Yes… I guess." Her belly was crawling with dread.

"I believe that one of the rules was about temper tantrums, wasn't it? And another about respect?" His voice was grim.

"I don't remember."

"GG."

"Yes, I guess they were. B-but I didn't really mean to…" She couldn't really think of a way to get out of it.

Leo took her by the hand and led her out of the bathroom and into the bedroom. He sat down on the chair and drew her to stand in front of him. "You know what comes now, don't you?"

GG squirmed and whined, "No, Leo, I don't want it."

"I imagine you don't. What comes now?"

She hung her head and said in barely more than a whisper, "I get a spanking."

Leo unbuttoned and unzipped her jeans and tugged them down over her hips to her knees. He drew her over to stand beside him and then pulled her down to lie across his lap. He laid a hand on her bottom and she felt the warmth of his big hand through her panties. Then he raised that hand and brought it down with a sharp swat, followed immediately by another swat on the other cheek. He spanked her for a couple of minutes and then stopped to pull her panties down. GG protested, but to no avail. He delivered hard smacks to her bare bottom, each slap leaving a fiery burn and quickly turning her cheeks red. Leo spanked her all over her bottom and then concentrated on the tender spot where her bottom met her thighs.

"Ow, ow, ow! Leo, stop, please! I'm sorry!"

The hard spanking continued and her bottom burned hotter with each painful smack. Then he moved down to the backs of her thighs. GG struggled harder, but that only resulted in Leo spanking her harder. When he went back to her sit spot, she burst into tears, sobbing her heart out. After a few more smacks, he stopped. She lay limp across his lap, wracked with sobs and he finally gathered her up and into his arms. She cried on his shoulder until there were no more tears left.

Finally, GG choked out, "I'm sorry; I really am."

Her husband put a gentle finger under her chin and raised her head to look her in the eyes. "What are you sorry for?"

Ashamed, she said, "I'm sorry I threw a tantrum. Everything you said was right, and I didn't want to hear it. I just wanted to be mad."

"Now, how about telling me exactly what was making you feel so bad? We need to talk about it when something's bothering you."

"I just...I was finished with all my housework, laundry, everything. Even the oven and the refrigerator are nice and clean. And it was only ten in the morning. And there wasn't anyone I could call or spend time with. Everybody is so busy and they're all doing things that are so worthwhile. They're working on degrees; you have yours and your new job, your *dream* job. All I've ever wanted is to see the world and to help people. Everybody else is working on doing it and all I'm doing is cleaning house and cooking. I'm a failure!"

Leo had the impulse to laugh a little, but he was quite sure that would be the wrong move. He thought it over for a minute and then said, "GG, I don't think you really understand what a help you already are to people. Do you think Katie would be in the spot she's in today if you hadn't stood up for her and become her friend? Maybe, but there's a good chance she wouldn't be. Your friendship turned her life around. And Sharon, you've been the best friend to her through everything. You supported her every minute that her brother was in Vietnam and they didn't know if every day might bring the worst possible news. Can you imagine how much she needed that? And there's Stevie. If it weren't for you, she could be on the streets with terrible things happening to her, or even worse. You're generous and kind and loyal and your friends know that. Look at the letters to the boys at the VA. Do you think I don't know that you're pretty much doing them all yourself now? Sharon and Katie are just too busy, but you're not about to let those boys down. And I can tell you just how much it means to them. You help everyone you touch."

GG was gazing at him, taking in every word. "You really mean that? Those seem like little things to me, just the normal things that anyone would do."

"I mean every word of it. And a lot of people wouldn't do it. They're little things to you because you have such a big, loving heart. I'm so proud of you. And the support that you give me is the best thing in my life. I know that I can count on you every minute of every day. Do you know how much that means?"

GG nodded slowly. "I guess I do because that's exactly what you give me. And it's the best thing in my life too."

Leo tilted up her head and kissed her tenderly. "I love you. And we're going to figure out what you would really like to do to fill up some of that extra time you have on your hands. Just so you keep cooking."

GG looked stricken. "Oh! Your dinner is sitting there getting cold."

Leo grinned. "I bet it's not that cold. Let's go eat."

GG discovered quickly that sitting to eat dinner was not the most comfortable thing after a spanking, but Leo brought her a cushion without saying a word, and just as he'd said, dinner wasn't that cold. She offered to heat everything back up, but Leo shook his head and dove right into his plateful of food, which was still warm enough as far as he was concerned.

After dinner, Leo read the Boone newspaper, which came out three times a week. His attention was captured by the community calendar of events and when GG was finished in the kitchen, he called her over and showed it to her. "Do you read this paper when it comes out?"

GG said, "I just kind of skim through the headlines and check out Mr. Vance's ad when it comes out on Wednesday. Why?"

"Look at this page, the community calendar."

GG looked at the section he was pointing out and said, "They have classes at the town center. I never knew that."

"You need to read that regularly. There are a lot of interesting things listed there."

GG was already absorbed in the calendar. "There's a painting class coming up. That would be fun. I wonder how much it costs to take the class."

"They have a phone number listed. Why don't you call tomorrow and get the details? I'm betting it's not going to cost much. And I'm also betting there'll be more interesting classes."

GG said, "You're probably right. Look, it says this month's arts and crafts class."

Leo urged her, "Call them."

"I will." GG impulsively threw her arms around her husband. "Thank you!"

He gave her an evil little smirk. "You mean for the spanking?"

"No! Well, maybe in a sort of roundabout way but, no, for helping me look for my hobby. And, mostly for what you said about me already helping people. I never really thought about it that way before."

"Well, I did. And I'm willing to bet a bunch of other people have too."

GG reached up for a kiss and said, "I love you, Leo Beauchamp."

"I love you back, Mrs. Beauchamp."

Chapter 7

G took her painting class and discovered that, although she loved it, she wasn't especially talented at it. But she did meet two women who were very talented and one of them gave her one of her paintings. GG was thrilled and Leo framed it for her so she could hang it up. The next class she took was pottery. Again, she loved it but her pieces were all a bit reminiscent of grade school art class. It was keeping her busy and, again, she met an artist who made a couple of really lovely pieces. She made friends with everyone she met in each of her arts and crafts classes, but she had an eye for spotting the really talented artists. The pottery bowl that her new friend gave her ended up on the console table they used for their keys, beside the front door. GG was busy and happy and had things to talk about besides her household chores and she took every class that she could.

In the middle of March, GG got up feeling a little off. She ignored it while she fixed breakfast and saw Leo off to work. After he left, she felt worse. She brewed a cup of tea and sipped it while she nibbled a piece of buttered toast. She felt a little steadier and set about cleaning up the kitchen when she suddenly was struck by a wave of intense nausea. She clapped her hand over her mouth and ran for the bathroom, where she retched into the toilet for several minutes. When she felt she could stand, she rinsed her mouth and splashed cold water on her face. She wiped her neck with a cool, damp cloth and felt better after a few minutes, until later in the day, when she ate half a sandwich and a cup of soup. She was fine for fifteen or twenty minutes, and then she repeated the same miserable performance she'd had earlier. When Leo got home, she was lying on the couch with her damp cloth draped over her forehead.

Alarmed, Leo asked, "GG, what's wrong? Are you all right?"

"I'm sure I will be, but I've felt miserable all day."

He knelt down beside her and felt her face, checking for fever. "What is it, exactly? Do you have a cold?"

"No, I just have a terrible upset stomach. Everything I ate today came right back up. I'm sure it's just a bug. I'll feel better in a day or two."

But she didn't. She would start out feeling good, but the nausea would hit her with no warning and nothing she tried to eat seemed to agree with her. After the third day, Leo insisted that she see the doctor. He took some time off work and went with her. After a thorough exam, the doctor told her to get dressed and then the nurse would bring them into his office. Leo and GG were terrified that something was seriously wrong. They sat in the chairs in front of the handsome desk in the doctor's office, waiting anxiously for him to come in. When he did, they were struck by the fact that he didn't look upset at all.

"Okay, you two. GG, I have a couple of questions for you."

Leo couldn't contain himself and he blurted out, "Doc, what is it? What's wrong with her?"

The doctor looked at him for a moment and said, "Well,

like I said, I have a few questions but I feel fairly confident in telling you that there's nothing wrong at all."

Leo and GG looked at each other, confused. "How can that be? She can't hold any food down."

"GG, when was your last period?"

It was the last question GG had been expecting and took her completely by surprise. "Um… I guess I'm not sure. I've been so busy, there's been so much going on."

The doctor smiled at her. "Well, I'll confirm it with the urine test, but I believe you're expecting. I'm not sure about dates. If you can pinpoint when your last period was, we can figure that out, but I'd say you've got a baby on the way."

GG was completely stunned but when she looked at her husband, the light was slowly dawning on his face and a huge smile took over the anxiety that had been there a moment before. Jumping up, he pulled her to her feet and wrapped his arms around her, laughing.

"A baby! GG, you're going to have a baby!"

"Oh, my God." She was instantly in tears.

"Baby, are you all right? Does something hurt?"

"Oh, Leo, we're going to have a baby! I can't believe it."

The doctor was sitting back in his chair, beaming at them. "If you'll have a seat again, I want to give you some written materials and go over some things with you."

It took a minute, but the happy couple finally settled back into their chairs. The doctor gave them a prescription for pre-natal vitamins and one for the nausea. He gave them the printed brochures he was talking about and gave GG some instructions about her diet and activities. And then he congrat-ulated them and sent them on their way. GG was busily thinking back and trying to figure out just when she had most likely gotten pregnant and Leo couldn't stop grinning.

"Leo, we weren't planning on this so soon. Are you really okay with it?"

"Baby, I'm so much more than okay with it, I don't even know how to tell you."

It was still sinking in to GG. "I just can't believe it. I always thought that a woman knows, she can feel it when it happens. I can't believe I didn't even have a clue."

"I'll take you home so you can rest and I'll go get your prescriptions filled. Are you feeling okay?"

"Leo, I feel fine. I can go with you to fill the prescriptions." GG was starting to feel the reality of it.

"Are you sure? I've got to take good care of you now." He was more than a little like a mother hen.

"Yes, I'm sure. Having a baby is a perfectly normal process. I'm not sick or frail. I have to take care of myself, but I don't have to act like an invalid." She had to laugh at him a little.

"It's so much to think about. We're going to have to have a baby bed and a high chair and… and everything!" Leo pulled into the parking lot at the pharmacy and turned to her. "GG, we're going to be parents." He said it in a tone of awe.

Suddenly her eyes were full of tears. "We are. We're really going to be parents."

"Oh, baby, don't cry." He put his arms around her and held her tenderly, patting her back.

"I'm just so happy." She let out a sob.

"I always thought that the day you married me was the happiest day I'd ever have, but this… this is more than anything I ever imagined."

"Oh, Leo. I love you so much. Our parents are going to be grandparents." The thought had just occurred to her.

He laughed. "They're in for a shock, aren't they?"

"Well, I can't say about your parents, but mine are going to be thrilled." She was beaming at the thought.

"So are mine. But I still think they're going to be shocked."

Before long, they were home with GG's prescriptions and

Leo was insisting on carrying her into the house. She laughed all the way in, and then he set her carefully on the couch and gently helped her off with her coat. He knelt in front of her and took her hands.

"GG, you've just made me the happiest man in the world. I don't know how to tell you exactly how I feel."

"But I know. It's how I feel too. It's the most amazing blessing I ever imagined. How did we ever get to be so lucky?"

Leo kissed her, a long, loving kiss that told her how much he loved her. "Are you all right? Are you hungry? Are you thirsty?"

GG laughed. "I could eat. Well, try to eat. Just let me go—"

"Absolutely not. You stay right here. I'm perfectly capable of getting my wife something to eat."

GG sat there, trying to fully comprehend the enormity of what was happening. She listened to Leo banging around in the kitchen, muttering under his breath now and then. He had propped her feet up on the ottoman, so she busied herself with looking through the pamphlets the doctor had given her and tried to tune him out. When he finally came back, he brought a tray that held a slightly overdone grilled cheese and a cup of chicken noodle soup, along with a glass of milk. GG looked suitably impressed and smiled as she took a bite of the grilled cheese.

"Mm. This is good. You're pretty handy in the kitchen."

"I lived on grilled cheese, fried egg sandwiches, and canned soup my first year of college. I got it down pretty well if I do say so myself." Leo grinned at her with just a little bit of pride.

"I'm going to examine the calendar so I can figure out how far along I am." GG sipped her milk and took another bite of her sandwich.

"When should we tell our parents?"

"Well, soon, of course. But I'd really like it if it could be just our secret for a couple of days. What do you think?"

"I think if that's what you want, that's what we'll do. It's just for us for now." Leo would have promised her the moon right then.

The doctor had told her that she could take one of the pills for nausea when she got home and then one each morning. One of the brochures was about morning sickness and it gave her tips on how to eat to help keep from having it so much. She was going to follow her instructions to the letter. Nothing was more important to her at this time than taking care of the baby she was carrying. After she finished eating, she asked Leo for the calendar and started out by filling in as many of the days as she could, thinking back on things she had done. It wasn't long until she let out a little cry of triumph.

Leo rushed in. "What's wrong? Are you all right?"

She was grinning at him. "Yes, I'm fine. I just figured out when I got pregnant. Come here; I'll show you." She went over the calendar with him, making sure he agreed with the days that certain things had happened.

"You're right. It was January fifth, the first Saturday in January."

GG was excited. "I'm two and a half months pregnant. That means I'll be due in October. Oh, Leo, we'll have a baby before Halloween."

"Can you figure out if it's a girl or a boy from that thing?"

GG laughed. "Nope, you're out of luck there. You're going to have to wait and see."

"My mom is going to be over the moon," Leo said.

"Mine too. We can't wait long. What if we invite everyone over for a potluck supper and tell them all then?"

"This place will be awfully crowded, but I like it. And I like potluck because you don't need to be cooking for that many people." Leo was relieved she had suggested it.

"I normally wouldn't mind doing it, but I just feel like I need to be a little bit careful."

"You're right. And, besides, potlucks are fun." Leo grinned at her. "We get more than one dessert that way."

"You're so silly. What do you think about Sunday? Is it too soon? Will they be okay with doing it on short notice?"

Leo assured her, "Of course, they will. And once they find out what it was for, they'll be thrilled to death."

"Okay. I'll call my parents and you call yours."

"Sounds good. Make sure Carl and Bryce know." Leo wanted to shout it to the world.

"We're in luck. Bryce is leaving in a couple of weeks for his new job."

"We need them all here. What about Sharon and Jack?"

GG nodded. "Why not? We can fit two more in."

"And Katie and Tommy?"

GG hesitated and then said, "I'm not sure…"

Leo dropped down beside her and took her hand. "If you ask me, I'm betting that Katie will be a lot happier that you include her than she would be if you left her out to spare her feelings."

GG gave him a luminous smile. "You're absolutely right, Leo Beauchamp. How did you get to be so smart?"

They were busy on the phone for well over an hour, evading the questions about what the occasion was, but when they were finished, they knew that all of them were coming.

"Did you eat?" GG asked suddenly.

"I had grilled cheese and soup too," Leo assured her.

"That's not enough for you, is it? There's some leftover ham in there."

"Ooh, I forgot about that. I'll make a sandwich. What about you? Are you still hungry?"

"I think I could eat a little bit. Like maybe half a sandwich." GG was surprised at how much better she felt.

"I'll make it," Leo said.

GG insisted on coming into the kitchen to eat with him and not more than an hour later, her eyes were getting heavy and she couldn't stop yawning.

"Come on, Mommy, let's get you to bed."

She melted at his words. "Mommy. I'm going to be a mommy."

GG fell peacefully to sleep on her beloved husband's shoulder, and he held her for a long time before he fell asleep. His protective instinct had never been so strong and he vowed to make sure that nothing ever happened to his wife and child.

Chapter 8

I t was a good thing Leo and GG only gave their families a couple of days' notice when they invited them over for the potluck. The whole family was buzzing with curiosity about what the occasion was. There was rampant speculation from the idea that the young couple had bought their first house all the way to maybe Leo had gotten a great job offer and they were going to move somewhere far away. The two mothers, especially, were suffering from intense curiosity. When nearly everyone arrived early on Sunday, Leo and GG looked at each other and acknowledged that they had to change their plan. They had planned on having everyone enjoy their dinner and then make the announcement. That was clearly not going to work. So they joined hands and faced their families while Leo called for their attention.

"We were planning to eat first and then talk, but y'all are dying of curiosity, aren't you?" There was a murmur of agreement. "So we're going to talk first and then we'll eat. All of this food looks amazing by the way."

"Well, get on with it, son, we're dying here!" Claire said impatiently.

Leo chuckled. "All right. Well, first of all, I heard some conversation to the effect of maybe we're moving away. That's not the case; we're staying right here in Boone for the foreseeable future." There was a ripple of approval in response to his words. "But things are going to get kind of crazy busy in our house."

"Did you get another job?" somebody called out.

"Did GG get a job?" came from someone else.

"It honestly doesn't have anything to do with any careers. The fact is… we're going to have a baby."

The house erupted into cheers, squeals of excitement, hands clapping, two moms weeping happy tears and dads clapping Leo on the back. There was mass confusion for several minutes as everybody in the house needed to hug and congratulate Leo and GG. As things calmed down a little, Leo looked over to see GG locked in her mother's arms, both of them with tears streaming down their faces. And then his mother wrapped him in her hug and Leo actually had to choke back a tear of his own at her reaction. Eventually, things calmed down, and after Leo's dad offered a prayer of thanks, they all raised their glasses and toasted the new life.

GG sat in a comfortable chair with her plate of food in her lap. She was feeling much better than she had before she'd had her visit with the doctor and she ate the delicious dishes everyone had brought and answered the many questions that her loved ones asked her. When Leo hovered over her a little too much, she laughed and sent him away to have a beer with the other men. GG was watching Katie surreptitiously, a little anxious over what her reaction would be, but Katie was all smiles, genuinely happy for her friend. Sharon was thrilled, although the idea of being a mother at such a young age shocked her a little. Molly and Ginny, Leo's sisters, were thrilled at the realization that they were going to be aunts. Bryce and Carl, GG's older brothers, teased her just like they always did, but in between teasing, they were beaming with pride.

When GG made her way back from one of her newly frequent bathroom breaks, her dad was waiting for her. She walked straight into his arms and he held her close for a full minute. "My little girl is going to be a mother. I can't believe it. I'm so happy for you, GG."

His words immediately made her tears flow again. "Thank you, Daddy. We're so happy too."

He held her hand and patted it. "You and Leo are going to make wonderful parents."

"It's a little scary," GG admitted.

Her dad's grin was huge. "Look at all the family you've got to help you. You're going to have way more good advice than you need, I'm sure."

GG laughed. "I didn't think about that, but I'm sure you're right. Look at the grandmas over there." Claire and Margot were deep in conversation and the excitement on their faces was obvious.

Don laughed too. "This is the best thing they've had to plan since you and Leo got engaged and they got to plan your wedding. Wait until you see your baby's first Christmas."

GG groaned. "Oh, my gosh, it's going to be crazy, isn't it?"

Her father nodded. "Count on it."

Bryce came over and slung an arm over GG's shoulders. "Hey, kid, how are you feeling?"

"I feel fine, how about you?"

In a moment of seriousness, he said, "I'm kind of wishing I wasn't leaving now."

GG said gently, "Bryce, this is your dream job. It's what you went to school for, what you worked so hard for. You have to go; I understand that."

Bryce had gone to school for journalism. He'd taken a double load of classes and worked summers interning for television news stations, and he was leaving in a few days for a job as an investigative reporter for a top quality news organization. "You'd better send me lots of pictures and letters."

"You'd better make sure you keep me up to date on your address."

"I promise," her brother said.

"I promise too," GG answered as he wrapped her in a hug.

The party went on until the food was pretty well wiped out. Everything was cleaned up without GG lifting a finger, and then their guests began to leave, a couple at a time. When the door finally closed behind the last of them, GG and Leo looked at each other with happy smiles. "I guess that was pretty much perfect," Leo said.

"It was. Everybody was so happy. It reminded me of our wedding." GG settled onto the couch, kicking her shoes off, and Leo brought her a glass of milk and settled down beside her to watch what was left of the football game. Within minutes, GG was stretched out on the couch with her head in her husband's lap, sound asleep. Leo looked down at her and the love he felt for her swelled inside him, stronger than he'd ever felt before. He pulled the afghan off the back of the couch and covered her gently. It was the perfect day and the perfect celebration of the life to come.

The next weeks were busy and happy. Leo made GG spend a day at her parents' house while he painted the spare bedroom a sunny yellow, so that she wouldn't breathe the paint fumes. By the time she got home, he was finished and had cleaned everything up and carefully aired out the whole house. She pronounced the room and the color perfect. They bought a crib at a garage sale and refinished it, ending up with a beautiful baby bed for their nursery. And Charles and Claire brought a gorgeous, handcrafted cradle that had been in the Beauchamp family for generations. They put it in the living room and Claire and Margot spent an entire day shopping for the softest and most perfect baby blankets to go in the cradle. By the middle of April, the nursery was nearly complete and GG spent a fair amount of time trying to keep the two grandmas from buying out the stores before the baby even arrived.

While things were happy and busy in Boone, Indiana, the unrest continued to grow in the rest of the country. The war was still raging and boys were still dying. There were still casualty reports on the evening news, and demonstrations for an end to it continued in cities and on college campuses. GG watched the news reports, read the newspapers and magazines, and wept at the loss of life and the increasing violence of the protests. It all came to a horrifying head in May, when the National Guard reportedly opened fire on students protesting at Kent State University, killing four and wounding nine.

Leo rushed into the house to find GG on her knees, weeping and staring in dreadful fascination at the live news on television. He gathered her up in his arms and carried her to the couch, where he held her and rocked her and bit back tears of his own. The news was terrible and the chaos at the Ohio university was shocking.

"I'll turn it off, baby," Leo murmured in her ear.

GG sobbed but said, "No. No, we have to watch. We all have to see. This can't go on; we all have to see it so we can stop it."

"Okay, baby, please don't be so upset." He knew it was a futile plea. There was no way to witness what was happening without being terribly upset.

They watched the news coverage for hours, and Leo got his wife to sip some chicken broth and a glass of milk by threatening to turn it off if she didn't eat something. She had just finished all the broth when Leo stiffened and exclaimed, "GG! That's Bryce! Look quick, right there with that photographer."

"Oh, my God, it *is* Bryce!" They were glued to the TV, and later in the evening, GG's brother actually spoke on the news broadcast.

Leo had called GG's parents, and the entire town of Boone was watching when one of their own reported from the scene of the awful happenings of the day. He had let his hair grow some; it was nearly to his shoulders and there was a rough stubble on his face. He looked the part of an investigative reporter and his family was proud of him even in the flood of grief they felt over the events of the day.

GG said, "He looks good, scruffy and maybe older, but good. Leo, he's going to see terrible things in the work he's chosen to do, isn't he?"

"He is. But he's driven to bring the truth to people. You know, most of the time, he covered it up with his joking, but he's really serious about it. He has a… a calling to bring the news to people. He talked to me about it one day."

"He did? I knew he was serious about it, but you know Bryce. He doesn't usually talk about serious things."

"No, but the serious side is definitely in there. I have a feeling that he's going to be very good at this. You can be proud of him." Leo hugged her close to him.

"I am. He was good when he spoke on there, wasn't he?"

"He sure was." They watched until the television stations went off the air for the night and then went to bed, where GG fell asleep from sheer exhaustion.

Leo lay awake for a while, thinking about the world their child was going to be born into. He had an enormous responsibility to protect his family, and that night it weighed heavily on him. They were living in some dark days, and he had an ominous feeling that there was worse to come.

Several days went by with a cloud over them, as if they were living through a bad dream. But life goes on, even after terrible things happen, and slowly people got back to feeling normal again. The protests went on, the war went on, and sometimes it seemed that none of it would ever end. But a week after the awful news from Ohio, a tragedy right there in Boone took over their lives.

GG was vacuuming the living room, her back aching. It had been aching all day and she was anxious to finish the chore and sit down with her feet up for a while. As she bent to unplug the vacuum cleaner, she was hit with a cramping pain that made her cry out and break out in a cold sweat. After a few seconds, it subsided and she sank into the nearest chair, trembling with her reaction to the sudden pain. She sat there for several minutes with no more pain, and she finally decided that it must have been a muscle cramp brought on by the vacuuming. She got up gingerly and finished putting the vacuum cleaner away, and then she doubled over with another pain.

"Oh, no, no, no, please." GG was weeping as she slowly made her way to the bathroom. Sure enough, she was bleeding. Not much, but enough to terrify her. As soon as she could, she called Leo.

"Baby, lie down on the couch with your feet up until I get there. I'm on my way."

Leo broke every speed law getting home, then he wrapped his wife in a blanket and carried her to the car. She was as white as a ghost and trying not to panic. Leo drove straight to the small hospital and carried her in through the emergency room entrance. Then the nurses and doctors took over, getting GG's doctor on the phone and getting her hooked to an IV. When they let Leo in, she was in a hospital gown, hooked up to an IV, and having her blood pressure monitored. Her doctor was on his way and it seemed like an eternity to Leo before he arrived. He came straight to GG's room and talked to her before he went to get out of his suit coat and into a lab coat and scrubs.

"Okay, GG, how are you feeling now? Any more pains?"

"No, not since that one when I first got here."

"All right, we're going to check everything out and see what's going on. Try not to worry; we're going to take good care of you."

But the doctor was not able to hear the baby's heartbeat, and by the next morning, GG had delivered a stillborn child. She sobbed so hysterically that they had to sedate her, and after, she had fallen into an exhausted sleep, Leo lowered his head to her bed and wept. He sat at her side, refusing coffee or water or any kind of comfort. GG cried in her sleep and Leo's heart was shattered, watching her. When she woke, he took her hand and did his best to comfort her.

"What did I do wrong?" GG asked.

"Oh, baby, you didn't do anything wrong."

"Maybe I shouldn't have been cleaning. Maybe I should have been more careful. Maybe I shouldn't have been watching the news like I did. It was so upsetting, maybe I shouldn't have…"

The doctor walked in and took a seat on the other side of her bed. "GG, there was nothing you did wrong and nothing you could have done to prevent this from happening. We don't know why it happens, but sometimes a baby just can't make it through pregnancy. You were completely healthy and you were taking care of yourself just as you should have. Something went wrong, but you didn't cause it. I've looked over every bit of your history and your medical records, before and during your pregnancy, and there's just nothing there. There's absolutely nothing to indicate that you can't have a normal, successful pregnancy when you're ready to try again."

GG's eyes were deep pools of pain. "How do I know that for sure?"

Her doctor said gently, "There's never going to be a guarantee, but sometimes we just have to have faith. Sometimes we have to take the risk if the reward is enough to be worth it. This is going to take time. You have to heal your heart, but if you want to try it again, I feel the odds are absolutely in your favor."

Leo looked overwhelmed at the idea that they could go through all of this again. But he would support his wife in anything she wanted to do. And, clearly, it wasn't something that they were ready to decide.

"Now, we can keep you here until tomorrow, just so you can rest, but if you want to, you can go home today."

"What about... what about my baby? What happens to him?

"That's up to you. Would you like to hold him?"

Leo sucked in a shocked breath. It was something that hadn't even occurred to him.

But GG was suddenly stronger. "Yes. I want to hold him. And I want to have him buried in our family gravesite. I don't want him to just disappear."

"All right. We'll get him ready and the nurse will let you know before we bring him to you."

When the doctor left the room, Leo said unevenly, "GG, are you sure?"

With tears in her eyes, GG said, "Yes. I can't say goodbye to him without ever seeing him. I'll never have another chance to hold him or touch him. I have to."

"All right." Leo didn't feel good about it at all, but he wouldn't have denied her anything at that moment.

But it turned out that GG had made the right decision for

them. They held their tiny, perfectly formed son and cried over him. They kissed him goodbye and smelled his little baby smell. The nurse offered to take some pictures for them to keep and when they finally let him go, they had said a real goodbye. GG took a sleeping pill then and Leo held her until she was asleep.

Chapter 9

Shelby was weeping quietly and her grandmother reached for her hand in wordless comfort.

"I'm so sorry, Gran. I can't imagine how much that hurt."

"No, I'm sorry, darling. I was so wrapped up in the memories, I didn't even think to prepare you for that. And there you are, almost ready to give birth to your first child. Please forgive me."

Shelby gave her a watery smile. "There's nothing to forgive. I wanted to record your life story. I knew it wouldn't all be happy and carefree. I'm just so sorry you had to go through that."

GG said, "It wasn't the only time it happened. We nearly gave up and then we were blessed with James. We thanked God every day for him and I still do."

"How did Katie handle it?" Shelby asked.

"Katie had a spine of steel, I swear. She held me and kept me going more times than I could count. And I know she felt basically the same pain I did. Even worse because she never once got to see or hold her baby. Katie was my rock and, of course, your grandfather. No matter how much pain he was in, he was always ready to comfort me. But enough of that. I'd say we need a lunch break, how about you?"

"We're always ready for food these days," Shelby said with a laugh. They had lunch and took a little walk afterward, then settled down to continue with GG's story.

Leo and GG named their baby after Leo's father and laid him to rest in the Boone Cemetery, where Leo's parents had bought a family plot for them, next to several generations of Beauchamps. They had a private graveside service for family and a few of their closest friends and everyone wept at the heartbreaking sight of the tiny white casket. GG's next pregnancy only lasted a few weeks before she miscarried, and that happened twice more. They put away the idea of having a child and went through a dark time. Leo immersed himself in his job and GG was pale and silent most of the time. Until Katie came to see her, once again, and this time, she scolded GG and shocked her into the realization that her life really wasn't over.

"What if you had let me keep walking around school, trying to fade into the woodwork and never talking to anybody? Where would I be now? Not becoming a nurse, that's for sure. I would have kept doing exactly what my mother wanted me to do and I wouldn't have any kind of life of my own. What's happened to you and Leo is terrible and I do understand how much it hurts, how it breaks your heart. You'll never, ever get over the pain, but you still have a life to live." Katie's words were fiery.

GG was shocked at first, then mad. She shouted back at Katie and then, looking horrified, she burst into deep, wracking sobs. Katie held her and cried with her, and when there were no more tears left, GG actually felt lighter. She knew it was going to hurt forever, but her friend was right and she had to go on. She knew she had been keeping Leo, the person she loved with all her heart, at arm's length and she was suddenly ashamed of herself. He was hurting too, and all she'd been thinking about was herself.

Katie was looking anxiously at her, wondering if she had gone too far, and when GG gave her a shaky smile, she let out a relieved sigh.

"Thank you, Katie. I needed that; I really did."

"You have no idea how glad I am to hear you say that. I was afraid I went way too far."

"No, it was just right. I've been all wrapped up in my own misery; I haven't even tried to help Leo. I think it's time for me to make it up to him. We should be closer than ever now, not further apart, and it's my fault." GG was suddenly seeing things much more clearly. She hugged Katie hard.

When Leo got home that evening, the house was full of delicious smells and there was music playing softly. Mystified, he walked to the kitchen, where he found his wife just taking her homemade peach crisp out of the oven. She set it down on a hot pad and turned to greet him with a smile and a kiss. He could hardly believe it was happening.

"How was your day? How's the project coming?"

She hadn't asked him about his day in weeks, and he dared to hope that his wife was back. She handed him a beer and listened to him tell her about his road project. Then he asked cautiously, "How was your day?"

"My day was good. Katie came to see me and we had a good talk. And then I realized that I hadn't made you your favorite dinner in a long time. So I went to Vance's and I've been in here since I got back."

Leo didn't have any idea what she and Katie had talked about, but he silently thanked Katie for it. When they sat down to dinner, it was the best tasting meal he could ever remember having. They sat together on the couch afterward and watched a little television, but they talked a lot. When they went to bed that night, instead of turning away from Leo, GG turned toward him and snuggled close. He held her close and she fell asleep with her head nestled on his shoulder and a heart that was a little more whole than it had been.

GG tried hard to put her heart and energy into the life she and Leo were making for themselves, although the ache in her heart was always there. She went to work part time for a little gift shop in Boone and kept on with her arts and crafts classes. When they got close to the holiday season, she began to realize that she really enjoyed working at the little shop. She talked the owner into putting some pieces of pottery in the shop that the artist she'd met in class had made. It turned out to be a good move and the pieces sold quickly. Soon her artist friend found herself busy turning out work to place in the shop.

It occurred to GG that she had met two other gifted artists in her painting class, so she looked them up and approached them to see if they'd like to put some work in the shop. Sure enough, one of them was really excited about the idea and the shop owner agreed to display some of her work, too. Through word of mouth, GG heard about a local candle-maker and went to see her. The little gift shop had the best holiday season of sales that it had ever had. GG was good with the customers and the artists and had a knack for finding exactly what appealed to most of the customers who came in to shop.

GG found that her busier schedule was good for her and good for her relationship with Leo. She had more to talk about with him instead of just listening to what was happening in his career. They had good holidays, although GG realized once Christmas was over, that she had enjoyed all the delicious meals and treats a little too much. Her jeans were a little tight and she realized she had gained a few pounds.

"Leo," GG said, frowning, "Look at this! I can barely button my jeans. I've got to lose a little weight!"

He leered at her. "I don't know, you look pretty delicious to me."

She had to laugh at him. "Obviously, I enjoyed all those holiday meals a little too much."

"I wouldn't worry about it. We're done eating that way for the season and you're busy all the time. You'll lose it in no time. I can help you exercise." He reached for her and cupped her butt in his hands, making her giggle.

But even though she was busier than ever, GG failed to lose the extra pounds. In fact, one day she stepped on the scale and realized that she had actually gained two more pounds. "Geez, GG, what are you doing? Turning into a chubby little housewife before you even turn twenty-one? That's it, you're going to live on salads until you get back in shape. Maybe you'll have to find a gym." So she made herself a big salad for dinner and only nibbled at the baked chicken that she made with it.

Leo held her close in bed that night and when he slid his hand up under her pajama top and fondled her breasts, it occurred to him that they felt a little more full. A thought occurred to him and he decided to keep it to himself for the time being. But he watched his wife and paid close attention to her actions for the next few days. She was getting sleepy a little earlier at night than usual and he grinned and teased her about winters being for hibernation. Nearly a month went by, and they were sitting at the table having dinner. GG was complaining about not being able to lose the stubborn pounds that were such a thorn in her side. Suddenly, she stopped and sat there, frozen. Her mind was obviously racing and Leo watched her face change, shock and a little dread passing across it.

"Leo," she choked out, "I think something happened."

He took her hand and said, "I know. I've been waiting for you to realize it."

Her eyes were huge. "You *knew*?"

"I suspected. I didn't want you to get scared. You're feeling good, aren't you?"

"I am. I haven't been the least bit sick. Is it really possible?"

He squeezed her hand and said, "I don't see why not."

"I need a calendar. I need to figure out…" She jumped up and went to their little office to get the calendar. She had to go back and figure out what they were doing and when, looking for clues that would help her with dates. "Leo, it's been more than four months."

He pulled her onto his lap and held her close. "How do you feel?"

"I feel good. Like, really good. It's weird."

"No, it's not. You've been taking good care of yourself and you haven't been worried about anything. You haven't been under any stress, and you've been busy with things that you really enjoy, right?"

She nodded slowly. "Yes, you're right." She laid her hands over her belly and realized that there was a tiny swelling there that she hadn't even paid attention to. She took his hand and laid it there and he could feel it too.

Leo gave her a long, tender kiss. "Tomorrow, we'll go see the doctor."

"And we'll keep it to ourselves. Until we know everything is okay. Even longer than that. It'll be our secret."

He kissed her again and said, "Agreed."

When Leo called the doctor's office, they immediately made time to see GG. When her exam was finished, the nurse brought Leo into the exam room, where Dr. Harper was ready to listen for a heartbeat. Leo held his wife's hand as the doctor listened intently and watched the smile spread across his face. After listening for what seemed like forever, he sat back and grinned at the excited young couple.

"Congratulations. There is no doubt that you are pregnant, GG, and your baby has a strong heartbeat. And I've looked at the dates you have written down here and I'd say you're right at twenty weeks."

GG burst into happy tears and Leo hugged her close. "I can't believe I didn't notice what was happening to me."

"Well, you know, you might have just refused to think about it. You've been through a lot and I understand how scary it would have been to be thinking about it right from the beginning. It could have been a way of protecting yourself until you reached the point where you are right now."

"So how do we make sure that nothing happens this time?" Leo asked.

"Okay, let's make a plan. I want you to eat well, sleep all you want to, start back on your vitamins immediately. Be reasonably active, just don't overdo it. No heavy lifting or heavy work of any kind. You work part time at the gift shop, right?"

"I do. Is that okay?" GG would have gone to bed for the rest of the pregnancy if he had told her that was best.

"I don't see why not. If you find yourself getting too tired, then cut back or quit if you feel it would be best. Let the way you feel guide you. And the same goes for when you're working; nothing heavy or strenuous. I'd say you should stop working six weeks before your due date, just to play it safe. Considering how you've been feeling up to this point, I'd say you're going to continue to feel good." Dr. Harper wanted nothing more than to see GG give birth to a strong, healthy baby.

Leo wanted to wrap his wife in a cocoon and hold her safe

until their baby arrived so he vowed to watch everything she did and help her as much as he could so that she wouldn't be taking any chances. "Are you sure it's okay for her to keep working?"

Dr. Harper chuckled. "As long as she doesn't overdo it, there's no reason she should have to quit. And there's one other thing you should know. You could feel your baby move at any time. You're far enough along, so don't be surprised. You might not feel it for a few more weeks, but it could be any day."

GG's eyes were huge and her tears spilled over again. "I can't wait! Oh, Leo, I just can't believe it."

"I'm going to have my nurse give you some printed material to read. There's a lot of helpful information and a list of things to watch for. I don't expect you to have any of those things happen, but if they would, call me right away. And, above all, relax and enjoy this pregnancy."

GG and Leo left the doctor's office in a bit of a daze. They went directly home and Leo fussed over GG until she had to tell him to stop. He had to go to work for the second half of his day, but he still had an hour to spend at home with his wife.

"How are you feeling?" he asked anxiously.

GG laughed. "Leo, I feel great! Except, I'm hungry."

"I'll get you something. What are you hungry for?"

"Stop. I can make us an early lunch. You need to eat before you go to work."

"Are you sure? I can do it. I don't mind at all."

"Leo, I love you. You're going to drive me crazy if you keep this up. Go get ready for work and I'll get lunch ready." She shooed him away after she gave him a kiss.

Leo went off to get dressed for work and had to take a minute to tamp down his anxiety. He grinned when he heard his wife singing while she bustled around the kitchen and the idea that they were going to be parents after all began to take hold of his heart. He walked up behind her in the kitchen and slid his arms around her, nuzzling her neck. She had warmed up some leftover chicken vegetable soup and made them some turkey sandwiches and they enjoyed the simple lunch as if it were a gourmet dinner.

"You remember what the doctor told you and don't do anything strenuous."

"I promise. Oh! Before you leave, you could take that basket of dirty clothes into the laundry room for me. This is going to take some getting used to." GG thought it was a little silly, given the fact that she'd been doing her housework up to this point with no harm done. But she wasn't about to take any chances with this precious pregnancy, so she would follow her doctor's instructions to the letter. She couldn't stop smiling and her hand returned again and again to the little baby bump at her waistline.

GG and Leo kept their treasured secret for another eight weeks by keeping busy and out of sight. But they finally began to run out of excuses to avoid their friends and family and, with Dr. Harper's professional opinion that there was no reason to keep it quiet any longer, they invited their parents over for a quiet dinner. Don and Margo were the first to arrive, and Leo opened the door to welcome them in. He took their coats and then led them to the kitchen, where GG was checking the lasagna in the oven.

"GG Beauchamp, I can't believe how long it's been since we saw you last!" Margo exclaimed.

GG laughed and straightened up, turning toward her mother. Margo looked at her and then her mouth dropped open in shock at the sight of her daughter, who was obviously pregnant.

"Oh, GG," she whispered and then wrapped her arms around her youngest child. She was crying happy, shocked tears, and it took Don a moment to comprehend what was happening. In a flash, his arms were around them both.

"I can't believe this! How far along are you?" Margo wiped away her tears.

"Six months, give or take a week or so. Oh! Mom, give me your hand." GG placed her mother's hand on her belly and a second later, they both felt the movement of the baby.

Margo gasped. "Oh, my word, that's my grandbaby moving around!"

The doorbell rang again and the whole scene was repeated for Leo's parents. Happy voices filled the room, and GG wasn't allowed to lift another finger to get dinner on the table once they had all felt the baby bump and exchanged hug after hug with lots of happy tears. It was a wonderful evening, and when the two sets of parents had gone home, Leo held his wife in his arms as his heart swelled with his love for her.

"This is going to be the best part of our lives together," he promised her.

GG snuggled against him and said, "Your lips to God's ears."

Chapter 10

G G's pregnancy went smoothly, with no resemblance to the terrible experiences she had had before. She took excellent care of herself and Leo watched over her like a real mother hen. And, of course, there were the grandmas and the aunts and uncles and, maybe the most doting of all, the grandpas. Katie and Sharon were both thrilled for her and threw her the best baby shower the town of Boone had ever seen. Lydia, the gift shop owner, watched over her too, and true to Dr. Harper's advice, GG gave up her job six weeks before her baby was due. She had a small library of books on giving birth, taking care of babies, natural child-birth, and story books that she read each night to her unborn child. She and Leo took a Lamaze class and she did her exercises and practiced her breathing faithfully.

On a beautiful, sunny day in late September, GG gave birth to a healthy, perfect eight pound baby boy. He had lots of dark hair and cried lustily until they gave him to his mother and she cuddled him to her breast. He quieted immediately and turned his little head, rooting for her nipple and eagerly taking her colostrum before falling peacefully asleep. The pregnancy had gone perfectly, just as the birth did, and when GG refused to let them keep him in the nursery overnight, Dr. Harper laughed and backed her up.

"It's been my experience that the mamas usually know best," he told the exasperated head nurse, and she threw up her hands and left the baby with his mother. Late the next afternoon, he told the proud parents that there was no reason they couldn't take their son home.

They named him James, after GG's great grandfather, and instead of a middle name, they only gave him the middle initial D, after both their fathers. GG's dad was Don and Leo's dad's middle name was David. Sharon and Katie came to visit as soon as GG gave them the okay, and Katie was stunned when GG asked her if she'd like to hold him. She had never held a new baby in her life, and as she sat there with him in her arms, a painful lump that had been in her heart ever since her baby was taken away broke apart and she felt free of it at long last. It was something that would always be with her, the pain of never knowing her child, but she was finally able to let go of the guilt. She had been a child, pregnant with a child, and she had given that child a home and a loving family. Her eyes shone with unshed tears as she smiled at GG.

"Are you all right?" GG asked anxiously.

Katie nodded. "I am. More all right than I've ever been before. Thank you, GG."

Sharon was watching with a smile, waiting patiently for her turn to hold the baby. She wasn't about to rush Katie; it was obvious that something was healing in her heart. When she finally held him, she couldn't stop smiling. The three of them cooed over his tiny fingers and toes and his long, dark lashes and deep blue eyes. He had GG's eyes and Leo's nose and chin and he was absolutely adorable. He was everything that GG had hoped for, and she had never been so happy in her life as she was when he was born. She had thought she could never be happier than the day she had married Leo, but giving birth to his son had been an even deeper happiness. Leo was right; this was going to be the best part of their lives.

Katie and Sharon had brought lunch. It was a pot of Sharon's mom's homemade beef and vegetable soup and freshly baked bread. They knew that GG was nursing her baby and Sharon's mom had nixed the idea the girls had of picking up cheeseburgers and fries from the Burger Barn. She informed the two of them that nutrition was very important to a nursing mother and happily made the soup for them. GG fed James while Katie and Sharon heated the soup and then the three of them sat down to lunch together.

"Tommy is talking about volunteering for the Peace Corps," Sharon said.

"Really?" GG was shocked.

"Yes, he's getting his journeyman's license in three months and he wants to do something meaningful, not just go out and make money," Katie explained.

"Wow, do you think he'll do it?" GG asked.

"I don't know. My mom hates the idea. He was gone for so long in Vietnam, and the Peace Corps can be dangerous too. If he could find a job as an electrician that also did something that would be helping other people, or maybe if he could work at his trade but also have something meaningful to do without going away... we just don't want to see him go," Sharon said pensively.

"I wonder if they need an electrician at the VA. He's a veteran, so he'd get preference over a civilian, I'm sure," GG offered.

Katie set her spoon down and said, "That's a good idea, GG. It can't hurt to ask, right? And I wanted to tell you that I'd like to start helping you with the letter writing again. I've gotten through the classes that I had to work really hard at, and I'll be done in a few months. And you're too busy with a new baby to do it all yourself. And I miss doing it, too."

GG grinned at her. "I have to admit, I'm glad to hear that. It's hard to believe that someone so little can cause me to be so busy."

"Do you need help with anything?" Sharon asked.

"No, honestly, between my mom and Leo's mom, I have more than enough help. Mom's been taking my laundry home with her and bringing it back all clean and folded, and Claire has brought dinner I don't know how many times. Leo insists that I nap when I can since I'm up a lot at night, so I'm enjoying it for now. It'll be all up to me and Leo soon enough. And it means that I can hold and cuddle my little guy as much as I want to, so I'm glad to have all their help. It'll be fun having help with the letters, though. I miss doing them together."

Sharon said, "I'll come as often as I can. I miss it too."

The three of them grew closer than ever as they got together each week to write their letters. Sometimes it took much longer than it ever used to, since they were busy cuddling the baby when he was awake, but they didn't mind that a bit. Leo would take him away whenever he was home, giving them time to write and him time with his son. By the time Christmas came, little James was laughing out loud when his daddy made faces at him or when his mommy played peekaboo with him.

The little family spent Christmas Eve with Leo's family and Christmas Day with GG's. They were just getting ready to sit down to Christmas dinner when they heard the back door open and a familiar voice call, "Merry Christmas! Where the hell is everybody?"

Pandemonium erupted as Bryce came through the door from the kitchen and Don wrapped his son in a bearhug.

Margo snapped, "Bryce Devereaux, is that snow on your boots?"

Bryce laughed and snatched her up, swinging her around and giving her a kiss on the cheek. "Merry Christmas, Mom."

"Oh, Bryce, you just made Christmas perfect. How did you pull it off? We thought you were out of the country."

"I was. I just made up my mind that I was going home for Christmas. I had some odd connections getting here, but I made it."

Carl was clapping him on the back and the twins shared their secret handshake, followed by a big hug, and then Bryce was looking around for his sister. When his eyes landed on her, standing at the far end of the dining room and holding her son, his grin stretched from ear to ear. A moment later, they were both wrapped in his arms. "Just look at you. You really are a mom."

GG couldn't help it; the tears traced down her cheeks as her brother saw his nephew for the first time. "I think he has your sense of humor," she said.

Bryce drank in the sight of him, and the baby took a firm hold on his finger. And then the baby laughed and the whole family was charmed. Margot was bustling around, setting another place at the table as Bryce congratulated the new daddy and James laughed at his uncle again. They finally took their seats and GG's dad offered a prayer of thanks for their many blessings. It was a wonderful dinner and they all ate too much and afterwards, Bryce held James on his lap and told him stories while the dishes were being done. GG found a quiet spot to sit and feed the baby where she could still hear the stories Bryce told of his adventures and the events he had covered. He only talked about the exciting or the funny ones, saving the tragic ones for another time.

The television was on, in honor of the football games that were being played that day. Margot shook her head in disapproval at the idea of football games on Christmas, but it was festive and fun. They ate ham and turkey sandwiches during the second game and later, as the game stretched on, they snacked on more pie and ice cream. Little James slept peacefully through the chaos, the talk and laughter, passed around from one set of arms to another. They took turns snapping picture after picture to commemorate the day. Bryce posed with everyone and, of course, everyone wanted a picture with the baby.

"How long will you be here, Bryce?" Leo asked.

"I've got four days before I have to fly out. So let's make the best of it."

"That's a promise," GG said. "I'll send you copies of all the pictures. And I've got baby pictures I can give you in person, since you're here."

"I have one of the three of you on my dresser, wherever I go," Bryce said. "And I keep all the letters I get from all of you. When I start missing home, I get them out and read some of them."

Carl said, "So why don't you tell us about the lady in your life?" He was digging for information.

Bryce laughed and said, "You mean ladies. My motto is have a good time and don't get serious. My lifestyle isn't exactly good for settling down."

Leo drawled, "Settling down is pretty darn good, the way I see it."

"Well, considering you're married to my sister, I'd say that's a good way to see it." They all laughed at Bryce's reply. "But getting shipped all over the world doesn't do a serious relationship any good, so I'll keep it on the light side. What about you, Carl? I figured you'd be all settled down by now."

"Nope." Carl shook his head. "Haven't found the right one yet."

"Well, I wish one of you would get on with it," their mother said. "I'm ready for more grandbabies."

Leo looked quickly at GG, but she was smiling peacefully at her son's face, and he relaxed. The Chiefs' quarterback threw the ball and a cheer went up in the Devereaux house, followed by a collective groan. Bryce got to his feet and headed to the kitchen. "I've got to have more of your cooking while I have the chance, Mom. I haven't had mashed potatoes since I left here."

Margot hopped up and said, "Let's heat you up a plate. I can show you my new microwave oven."

"Your what?" Bryce asked as the two of them disappeared into the kitchen.

Carl was rolling his eyes and laughing. "Bryce is going to get the microwave demonstration. I swear, she loves that thing."

"She does," Don affirmed. "I have to admit, it's pretty handy to warm up leftovers."

Leo said, "They're saying that in no time, every household will have one."

"No way," said Carl. "They say someday everybody is going to have a phone in their car, too, but I don't believe it."

They all laughed and GG said, "A phone in the car could be a good thing."

Carl said, "It could, but that doesn't mean it's going to happen."

Bryce came back with a plateful of food and GG groaned at him. "I can't believe you're still hungry!"

"Hey, I haven't had cooking like this in months. I'm stuffing myself with it as much as I can while I'm here." He gave her a grin and a wink as he took a bite of sweet potatoes. "How's school going, brainiac?" His question was directed at Carl.

"It's going great. I'm working on my Master's. I finally feel like the end of my school days is approaching." Carl was studying to be a prosthetics designer.

"About time you started earning a living." Bryce grinned at him. "No wonder you haven't found the right lady yet. Your nose is always in the books."

Carl laughed at him. "All in good time."

"Leo, are you liking your job?"

"I love my job," Leo said. "It's everything I hoped for when I finally got through with school."

GG smiled at him proudly and Bryce turned his attention to her. "And you have the best job of any of us, don't you, sis?"

"I think so," GG said. "There's nothing I'd rather do than be Mommy."

"I want to come visit you and spend a little more time with the little guy," Bryce said.

"I'd love that! I can cook you dinner," GG said.

"Sounds good, but I'll come a couple of hours before dinnertime so we can have plenty of time. Is tomorrow okay?"

"Of course." GG was thrilled that he would be coming. "We usually eat at six, but tomorrow's Sunday, so come when-ever you're ready."

"Okay, I'll give you a call tomorrow and give you a head's up before I leave here."

Leo and GG stayed later than they had planned, reluctant to leave with Bryce there, but eventually GG could barely keep her eyes open and they had to go. When they snuggled together in bed that night, GG gave a happy sigh and said, "It's so good to have him home."

"Pretty great Christmas present, wasn't it?" Leo asked, kissing the top of her head.

"This is the best Christmas ever." GG lifted her head for a real kiss. In no more than five minutes, she was sound asleep in her husband's arms.

Chapter 11

Bryce arrived in the middle of the afternoon and GG and Leo showed him around their little house. He made them laugh when he described the tiny apartment he'd been living in while working in Spain, where he was covering a story about a terrorism investigation. It was barely more than a room and there was a shared bathroom. His descriptions were so vivid that GG could almost hear the sounds and smell the smells of the neighborhood he lived in.

Bryce held the baby while they sat and talked. GG had her beef stew in the oven, fresh bread already baked, and a pan of her peach crisp ready to serve. Leo and Bryce had a beer and GG sipped a glass of lemonade. She couldn't get enough of her brother's stories, but after she fed and laid James down, sound asleep, he grew serious.

"I need to tell you something, sis. I wanted to tell you first, so you can help me with Mom."

GG got an uneasy feeling. "What do you mean, help you with Mom?"

"She's not going to like it, and I've got to try to make her understand. So I really need your help."

"Bryce, what have you done?"

Bryce hesitated for a moment and then said, "I'm going to be starting a new assignment. I applied for credentials and got them, to cover the conflict in Vietnam. I'm going to Saigon."

GG's face turned white and she gasped in shock. "Bryce! Why? Why would you do that?"

He leaned forward and said earnestly, "GG, I have to. It's the most important story going on in the whole world and I need to cover it. It's the chance of a lifetime, as far as my career goes, but it's really that I *need* to see the truth and tell it to the world."

"Oh, Bryce, don't you remember how Mom—how all of us—prayed, day after day, that you and Carl wouldn't have to go? I can't believe that you actually *want* to go to that awful place." GG's voice was trembling and she was getting angry.

"Easy, GG," Leo said soothingly.

"Easy, my ass! I can't believe this is happening. How am I supposed to help you with Mom? *I* don't want you going over there! This is going to break Mom's heart; you know that. Why didn't you tell Carl? He's your twin." GG was so upset that she was shaking.

"Carl knows. But you're the one who can soothe Mom; you and Dad. Please, GG, I really need you to be on my side."

"That's not fair, Bryce. You really want me to be okay with this?"

"I really want you to support me. It's going to be hard, and I can't say that it's not scary. I need my family to be behind me. Don't be mad, sis. If I didn't believe that I have something important to do there, I wouldn't go. But I have to. It's that simple."

GG could see that he was telling her the truth as he saw it. And she obviously wasn't going to convince him not to go. She wasn't really angry at him; she was just plain scared. "It's so dangerous there. How many journalists have been killed or just disappeared over there?"

"There have been some," Bryce admitted. "I'm going to be as careful as I can. I'm not going to take stupid chances, but I have to do it."

GG stared at him for a long time, then she turned her back and paced the room a few times. When she whirled around to face him, her expression was fierce. "Bryce Devereaux, don't you dare let anything happen to you! I'll never forgive you if you go over there and get yourself killed."

He crossed the room and wrapped his arms around her. "I promise. I'm coming home from there once my job is done. I promise. Don't cry. It's going to be okay."

GG dashed away her tears and said, "I'm holding you to that promise. Don't you dare let me down."

"Not a chance. Besides, I've got to watch your little man grow up, right?"

Leo had watched them without saying a word. He walked over and put an arm around his wife's shoulders and held a hand out to Bryce, who gripped it hard. "Be damn careful over there. Journalists are housed in Saigon, right?"

The three of them moved to the kitchen to sit around the table and talk. Bryce said, "That's right. Stories have to be sent from Saigon back to the U.S. or telephoned from a U.S. base. You can go pretty much anywhere with our troops, but you need to get back to Saigon to file your stories."

They talked for a long time, until James woke up and GG went to change and feed him. Leo and Bryce talked in more detail about the jungle he was going to while GG was busy with the baby. Leo could understand his need to go, but he knew the kind of shock it was going to be when he actually got there. He also suspected that there was an element of danger that was at least a little bit of a thrill for a man who did what Bryce did for a living. When GG came back to the kitchen with the baby, they dropped their conversation.

"When are you going to tell Mom and Dad?" GG asked.

"I figure I'd better do it when I get back there. They'll be pissed if I don't tell them as soon as possible. They'll probably be pissed that I haven't already done it and I can't really blame them. Will you go with me?"

GG gazed solemnly at him for a minute then nodded with a sigh. "Yes, I don't really know what I can do, but I'll be there, and I'll try."

"Thanks, sis. I owe you one."

"Yeah, a big one. Who's hungry?"

Leo said, "I'm starving! That stew smells so good, my stomach's been growling for an hour."

"I'm always starving," Bryce said with a grin.

"You guys bring the baby's cradle in here and I'll get dinner on the table."

"Yes, ma'am," her husband said.

Bryce held the baby until GG was finished and then Leo settled him in the cradle and they sat down to eat. Leo said a prayer and they ate and talked, with both men having second helpings of GG's stew. After dinner, they did the dishes and then they all went to GG's parents' house. When they all trooped into the house, Margot was in her glory. Her whole family together at Christmas time was a wonderful treat for her. She wasn't going to be happy for long. When Bryce broke the news to his parents, his mother's reaction was instantly angry.

"No! No, Bryce, you are absolutely not going to that horrible place! I won't have it. Don, tell him, he's not going." Margot's face was red and she was nearly shouting.

"Now, Margot, calm down. Let's talk about this. Let's hear Bryce out. He's not a boy anymore, and I know he has reasons for this decision." Don was soothing but firm.

She stared at her husband in disbelief. "You can't be serious. I don't care what his reasons are. People get killed over there every minute of every day! *Journalists* get killed over there!"

"That's enough!" Now Don was more than just firm and, astonishingly, his wife didn't say another word. "Bryce, tell us about all this."

So Bryce told them about the way he had felt more and more strongly that there was a story there that was important for him to see and him to tell. For the first time, his mother heard exactly how much passion he had for his profession. He told them about the process of applying for credentials and how surprised he had been when he'd been approved. He told them what he knew about the daily routines of the war correspondents in the country, about the headquarters in Saigon, about having to be there every night to transfer his stories to the United States. He didn't tell them that journalists routinely hitched a ride on a chopper to the war front to be in the actual action, but they had seen the pictures and Don, at least, had a good idea of just how close they got to the fighting. He told them just what he had told GG, that he felt he had to go and he told them how much he needed their support.

Finally, GG went to her mother and took her hand. "Mom, I know what you're feeling, I felt the same way. But he's really going to do it and he needs us. And he promised me that he's going to come home safe. He promised me and James."

Her mother sniffed. "Oh, and I suppose you think he knows he can actually pull that off. He can't see the future and he can't control what happens over there."

"No, but if he promised, then he's going to do the very best he can to see that he does. The thing is he's going to go and we can't let him leave with us mad at him."

That made her mother's face soften, and tears welled up in

her eyes. "Don't make me see it fairly. I don't want to. I don't want him to go."

"I don't either, but we don't get to choose."

"Oh, GG... damn it, Bryce, why couldn't you have been a schoolteacher? Or a-a librarian, for God's sake!"

"Geez, Mom," Bryce protested.

Somehow, everyone found a little laugh at the silliness of her suggestions and the tension was broken. They began to ask Bryce questions about what he was going to be doing, where he was going to be living, when he was going to leave for Vietnam and how long it would take for him to get there. He had a picture of the building in Saigon where he would be spending a lot of time and he told them about the photographer who would be going with him. He tried hard not to be too enthusiastic about what he was undertaking, but nobody could miss the spark in his eyes when he talked about it. Watching his son, Don acknowledged silently that he was an adventurer. They would have been as successful at stopping a train as they would at stopping Bryce from taking this assignment.

Leo gave his wife a hug and leaned to give her a quick kiss on the cheek. When she looked at him questioningly, he winked and said softly, "I'm proud of you."

The Devereaux family spent every minute they could of Bryce's time there together. He promised to get his address to them as soon as he had it. He took photographs with him and all their love and best wishes. They took him to the airport in Indianapolis and watched until his plane was in the air. And then they went quietly home, each with a little hole in their heart. GG cried a little on Leo's shoulder and Margot did the same on Don's shoulder when they went to bed that night. It was a new chapter in their lives and they just hoped it wouldn't end badly.

Several months went by and the Devereaux and Beauchamp families got used to Bryce being gone, at least as much as they could. Life was busy for them all. Tommy got his journeyman's card and GG and Sharon arranged for him to talk to the proper people at the VA. They didn't hire him, but they did introduce him to a disabled veteran who had been an electrician by trade before he was wounded in Vietnam. He hadn't been able to work at his trade, not because he was completely unable, but because there were certain things he couldn't do and that kept him from taking on jobs. Together, the two of them created a successful partnership and Tommy got the satisfaction of helping a fellow veteran.

Katie graduated from nursing school and went to work at a clinic south of Indianapolis. She spent one Saturday every month at the shelter that GG had taken Stevie to, assisting a female doctor from her clinic who volunteered her services to the women in the shelter. Stevie was working part time at an animal shelter and caring for the frightened, lonely animals suited her perfectly. She looked nearly like the old Stevie, but with a wariness in her eyes that would never go away. She had moved to an apartment in a cozy house that had been converted to four separate apartments, run by the cheerful sixty-year-old woman who had lived there with her husband until he passed away several years before.

GG wrote to her brother every week, sometimes twice, and sent him lots of pictures of James, who took his first steps by himself in May. He was a happy little boy with a sunny disposition, and he was the joy of both families. Katie came every other Sunday afternoon to write letters with GG, since she wasn't living in Boone anymore. Sharon came once or twice a month, as she was finally in law school. In midsummer, Sharon showed up with an extra happy glow on her face. She laughed when James ran to her with his arms up and telling her his whole life's story in his baby babble.

GG said, "Well, you're awfully happy today. What's going on?"

Sharon was cuddling James on her lap, and she tried to act nonchalant but couldn't hold it in. "Look!" She held out her left hand, where an absolutely beautiful chunk of diamond sparkled. "I'm engaged!"

GG squealed in excitement and hugged her friend tight, making James laugh from where he was squashed between them. "Congratulations! I was beginning to think that you two were never going to get around to this! It *is* Jack, right?"

Sharon burst into laughter and said, "Of course, it is. You know that. And we've been busy, you know. Med school, law school, it's hard to find time for little things like getting married."

"Oh, Shar, I'm so happy for you!"

Just then, there was a tap at the door and then Katie walked in. "Well, what the heck is going on here?"

James was shouting, "Kay! Kay!" and Sharon and GG were talking at the same time. Finally, Katie's eyes lit on the big diamond and she let out a squeal of her own. She and GG hugged each other and danced around, babbling excitedly while James watched them with wide eyes.

"Oh my gosh, Sharon, congratulations!" Katie was thrilled for her.

"Thank you, thank you," she said from her seat with James on her lap.

The baby held his arms out to Katie and she took a turn holding him. GG gave Sharon a hard hug, wiped away a happy tear and said, "This calls for a celebration! I know. Ice cream!"

"Perfect," said Sharon.

Just then, Leo came in from the back yard, where he had

been trimming some bushes and said, "What the heck is going on in here? Y'all are making enough noise to wake the neighbors."

"Look!" GG grabbed Sharon's hand and held it out toward him.

"Wow! That's not the one he showed me."

Sharon's mouth dropped open and she said, "He *showed* you one?"

Leo said innocently, "Yeah, it wasn't nearly as big as that one."

"What? Are you serious?"

Leo laughed. "No, I'm just kidding. Congratulations to both of you."

They all laughed at the look on Sharon's face and James laughed at all of them. GG said, "We were just deciding on how to celebrate. We thought maybe ice cream."

"Well, why don't you let me take this guy and you three go to the Burger Barn for milkshakes?"

GG dimpled up at him. "Aw, that would be great. Want me to bring you something?"

"Absolutely. My usual would be perfect."

So the three women went to the Burger Barn and celebrated with French fries and milkshakes and GG brought home a double cheeseburger, fries, and a chocolate shake for her husband, who shared his fries with his son. They dashed off their letters and when Sharon and Katie left, they were all tired but happy. It was a good day and GG's heart was full as she watched her son sleep, his little arm tucked around his favorite stuffed puppy and his thumb in his mouth.

Chapter 12

G G was still writing faithfully to her brother once or twice a week. Sometimes he wrote back and sometimes he didn't, but she knew that he did when he could. In September, when she and Leo were getting ready for James' first birthday, he sent a long letter, catching up on the time that had flown by since he'd left. He sounded lonely when he wished his little nephew a happy birthday, and GG's heart ached for him. He told her that tensions had escalated and assured her that he was being even more careful than ever. They watched the news faithfully and sometimes got to see him. He was thin, and his hair was long, as usual, and he was crisp and concise in his reporting.

In December, peace talks between the United States and North Vietnam collapsed and President Nixon began a bomb campaign beginning on December 18th. Over 20,000 tons of bombs were dropped on the cities of Hanoi and Haiphong. The U.S. lost a number of B-52s and other aircraft as the bombings continued through Christmas until the 29th of December. The North Vietnamese finally agreed to resume the peace talks, and a few weeks later, a final peace treaty was signed and the war officially came to a close. In January of 1973, the draft in the United States ended.

Still, journalists remained in Vietnam and Bryce didn't come home. He wasn't answering GG's letters as often as he had before, and it was the same with his letters to his mother. Finally, in late April, GG received a brief letter that told her he was coming home and bringing a surprise. He didn't offer any other details and the family waited impatiently to hear more from him. One day in mid-May, GG got a phone call from him. The connection was scratchy and he had to practically shout at her, but he let her know that he was on his way home. He said that travel would take a couple of days and he would call her when he arrived in the States. And he told her to keep it to herself, so he could surprise the rest of the family.

GG hung up and hugged herself in relieved delight. Leo was at work and James was napping, so she had no one to tell her good news to. By the time Leo got home, she was bursting with the need to share it with him. He swept her up into a hug and then swept James up with them, dancing them around in a circle. They celebrated by ordering pizza for dinner, which was James' favorite treat, and then read him two books at bedtime. Later, they laughed softly together at how their lives had changed.

"I like that happy look in your eyes," Leo said, toying with her hair.

She snuggled close to him. "It feels so good, to know he's coming home safe."

Leo pulled his wife down onto his lap and stroked her hair, turning her face to his for a kiss. She murmured softly and he unbuttoned the first couple of buttons of her shirt, stroking her lightly. GG responded by unbuttoning his shirt and placing her hands on his chest, stroking the muscles of his shoulders and down to his hard belly. Leo slipped his fingers into her bra, finding her nipple hard and aching for him. He picked her up and carried her to the bedroom, where he undressed her, one article of clothing at a time. He took his time with each bit of skin that he exposed, touching, stroking, tasting her. Her skin was so soft and smooth, he never got tired of touching her, or looking at her, for that matter.

GG squirmed under his hands, her body responding to every touch. She gasped and her back arched as he lowered his mouth to the swollen, rosy peaks of her breasts. He licked and sucked one, then the other, pulling it into his mouth and worrying it with his tongue while his hands teased her, pulling lightly at the soft down between her legs and just barely stroking the swollen folds between them. GG pushed up against his hand, aching for his touch, and gripping his buttocks to pull him against her. He chuckled at her and made her wait, still teasing. He nipped and licked at her, then he turned her over on her belly and trailed kisses down her spine, nibbling at the sensitive spot just under her lowest rib and making her shiver in delight. He spread her legs and danced his fingers lightly between them, feeling how hot and wet she was. When he slowly pushed a finger up into her tight heat, she gave a groan of pure animal desire.

"GG, what is it that you want?" he murmured in her ear.

"I want you, Leo," she gasped the words at him.

He bit her perfect, round butt cheek lightly, making her gasp again, and pushed a second finger up into her. He thrust his fingers in, withdrew, then thrust again while he rubbed the hard little bud that gave her so much pleasure with his thumb. GG bucked against his hand as he drove her closer and closer to orgasm. And then he stopped. He pulled his hand away and turned her back over on her back, spreading her legs wide. Leo laid his erect manhood against her wet, swollen center and rubbed against her lightly.

"Leo, please," she begged, "don't make me wait any longer. Please."

In one smooth, fierce thrust, he was deep inside her. She gave a guttural moan and rose to meet him. They moved together in a rhythm that was only theirs, harder and deeper with each rocking thrust. GG had to press her hand against her mouth to swallow a scream as she soared to a shattering climax. The hard contractions of her muscles drove Leo to his own climax and they shuddered together, quaking with the force of their union. They lay together, breathing hard and quivering with lovely little aftershocks of pleasure.

"Oh, Leo, I love you so much," GG murmured the words into his ear.

His grip on her tightened and he said, "Not any more than I love you." They fell asleep in each other's arms and James accommodated them by sleeping straight through the night.

The next day dragged by with no word from Bryce, as did the day after that. On the third day, she was finally blessed with the call she was waiting for. It was late in the afternoon, almost time for Leo to get home from work, and Bryce told her he had just landed in Indianapolis.

"See? I kept my promise," he said with a laugh. "I'm going to get a room here. I'm beat; it's been a long couple of days. I'll rent a car in the morning and drive to Boone. So I'll be at your place by lunchtime."

GG pouted a little. "That's so long from now."

He laughed at her. "It's been over a year. I think we can make it until tomorrow."

She stuck her tongue out at him, even though he couldn't see her. "Okay, you're right. I'll see you tomorrow by lunchtime. Hey, what's the surprise you said you're bringing?"

"Oh, no, you'll have to wait until tomorrow to find out about that. I love you, sis. See you tomorrow."

GG hung up the phone and picked up her son, dancing around with him and making him laugh hysterically. She gave him a loud, smacking kiss on the cheek, which made him laugh harder, and beamed at him. "Your Uncle Bryce will be here tomorrow! What should we do special for him?"

She settled for making sure that the house was spotless, even though she had cleaned it from top to bottom every day since Bryce had called. When Leo got home, she excitedly told him her news. She was so excited that she even had a sip of Leo's beer, though she didn't really like it that much. She was up early in the morning and by ten, she had made potato salad and macaroni salad and baked a pan of brownies. She had assorted cold cuts for sandwiches and both iced tea and fresh lemonade in the refrigerator. Leo took half a day off work and got home a few minutes before noon. Not more than fifteen minutes later, they heard a car in the driveway.

GG ran to the door and flung it open, words of greeting on her lips that died suddenly when she saw her brother open the passenger's door and a slender, dark haired girl take his hand and climb out of the car. He said something to her and she smiled up at him before they turned to come toward the house. GG had never been so shocked in her life; the girl was clearly pregnant.

When Bryce saw her in the doorway, he got a worried, uncertain look on his face. He went to her quickly and wrapped her in a hug.

"Wow," she said shakily. "You weren't kidding when you said you had a surprise."

Bryce turned and held his hand out to the girl. "GG, this is my wife, Quyen. Quyen, this is my sister, GG."

The lovely Vietnamese girl dipped her head shyly and said, "It is very good to meet you."

With only a second's hesitation, GG took both of her hands and said, "It's wonderful to meet you. Come in; meet my husband and our son."

The introductions made, they sat down together to talk for a little bit. Bryce decided that the best thing was to meet the elephant in the room straight on. "I met Quyen near Hanoi, just before the bombing started. I knew it was coming, so I took her back to Saigon with me. She has no immediate family and her more distant family was far away. Quyen was in love with an American G.I. and he was trying to get approval from the Army to get married. But it's a very slow process and he never made it back to get her. I was trying to trace what happened to him, but haven't found out anything yet. As you can see, Quyen needed a protector, someone to look out for her. So the simple answer was to marry her and bring her back here."

GG didn't know what to say. It was so clearly not simple at all, but she could understand the strange logic that had brought Bryce to that conclusion. "Well. I'm not sure it's as simple as you're saying, Bryce, but you're welcome here, Quyen. Please don't feel uncomfortable."

Quyen gave her a little smile and seemed to relax just a tiny bit. "Thank you, GG. I am happy to be here."

"Your name is beautiful. What does it mean?"

She smiled a little self-consciously. "It means bird."

"That's lovely."

Leo put James down on the floor and he walked over to Bryce and Quyen and then gave his sunny little smile and held his arms out to Quyen. Her face lit up with pure happiness and she glanced at Bryce and then GG for permission. When GG smiled and nodded, she scooped James up and sat him on her knee.

GG laughed. "James loves to meet new people. He's not exactly shy, as you can see."

Quyen's laugh was musical and GG was just a little enchanted. It was a helluva surprise and GG couldn't imagine what her mother's reaction was going to be, but she already liked Bryce's new wife. But this was going to shake up her family; not because of who Quyen was but what the situation was. She needed to talk a lot more to Bryce. What were his plans? He talked as if he was searching for the American that Quyen had fallen in love with, but if he wanted to do that, marrying her himself didn't make sense. If he had married her just to provide her with protection, then that told her that he wasn't in love with his wife. What would he do if he found the man? Was he planning all along to divorce her? And what about the child? GG grew more concerned and confused, the more she thought about it.

After lunch, GG cornered Bryce in the kitchen, asking him to help her with something. Leo took the hint and took Quyen to see the baby's room. "Bryce, are you really going to spring this on Mom and Dad the way you did on us? Don't you think you should go talk to them first?"

He gave her a wink and a grin and said, "I said I was bringing a surprise." He sobered at the look on her face. "Honestly, it's not going to make it any easier. And I'm hoping when they see her, it'll soften them up."

"You know perfectly well that they'd never be anything but nice to her. But you've got yourself in a really strange spot, don't you?"

"It's not exactly the way I told you, but we'll have to talk about it more later, when we've got some privacy. I just want to get through this and then figure out what to do next." He had a bit of a stubborn look on his face and GG knew his mind was made up.

She sighed, not a bit less worried. "Okay, good luck."

Bryce looked alarmed. "You're going with us, right?"

GG gave him a withering look. "I should say no."

"But don't. Please."

"You're impossible. Okay, we'll go. But you've got a lot of explaining to do."

"I will, I promise."

GG was right; there was a real shockwave through the

Devereaux household when Bryce walked in and introduced his bride. Even Carl was visibly shocked. Bryce gave them the same explanation that he had given to GG and Leo, and GG could see that none of them bought it. As she had expected, her parents were nothing but kind and polite to Quyen, but their concern was obvious too. GG went into the kitchen with her mother to get some drinks and her mom whirled around as soon as they were out of sight of the rest of them.

"What in God's name was he thinking?" Margot's tone was fierce, but she kept her voice down. "What's he doing? He says she just needed a protector and someone to help her out, so he *married* her? GG, she's having a *baby!* Is he a husband to her, or was it just to get her out of the country and into the United States?"

GG shrugged helplessly. "I don't know, Mom. He hasn't told us any more than he told you. But none of it makes any sense."

Her mother said, "He's going to be the death of me. And that poor girl! If it's not a real marriage, what's going to happen to her and her child?"

GG gave her mom a hug. "You're such a good person, Mom. I guess it'll all work out somehow. Maybe it'll make more sense once we hear the whole story."

"I sure hope so because it doesn't make a bit of sense right now." The two of them carried the drinks out to the living room and rejoined the rest of the family.

Bryce was explaining that they had a room at the Boone Inn and his mother never attempted to get them to stay with his family. She was going to need to hear his explanation before she could get anywhere near to feeling comfortable with his new relationship. And it was a few days before his explanations were forthcoming. In the meantime, Bryce spent his time getting a doctor's appointment for Quyen and looking at the possibilities of where he could be working next. Finally, he arranged to visit GG without bringing his wife.

"The heavy bombing was just starting and I wasn't too far from where they were striking. Quyen was hiding, terrified. Her family disowned her and kicked her out and she had nowhere to go, nobody to help her. I couldn't just leave her there."

"Why did they disown her?" GG was shocked once again.

"Because she fell in love with an American and, even worse, she got pregnant. He went back to the States and promised that he'd be back for her. When he left, she must have just gotten pregnant, because she waited for a few months without her family knowing about the baby. It was when the bombing first started that they threw her out."

"They threw their daughter out when the bombs were falling?" GG was horrified.

"Yes. As far as they were concerned, she wasn't their daughter anymore."

"Oh, my God. What happened to the soldier she was involved with?"

Bryce shrugged. "He probably went home and went on with his life."

"He just dumped her? After he promised to come back for her?"

"It happened a lot. And, to be fair, he didn't have any idea she was pregnant when he left. But it probably wouldn't have made any difference." Bryce's words were both cynical and matter-of-fact.

"That's terrible. But, Bryce, you *married* her!"

"It was the easiest way to get her out of there."

"So… is it a real marriage?"

He gave her a grim smile. "There's no physical relationship between us."

"Oh, Bryce. Then, what are you going to do next? What was your plan?"

"I figured I'd bring her here, find a place to set her up where she'd be safe. Help her get a start and, once enough time goes by that she can stay here, we could get divorced."

GG was speechless for a full minute. "That's the dumbest plan I've ever heard," she scolded. "Does she know about this plan?"

Her brother shifted uncomfortably. "Well, not exactly. She thinks I'm going to try to find the guy, then we can get divorced and they can get married."

GG groaned. "But you know that's not going to happen."

"I guess nothing is totally impossible, but I'm pretty sure, yeah."

"So now what are you going to do? You're going to be moving off to your next assignment soon. Are you going to take her with you? Behave like she's really your wife? Because, she is, you know."

Bryce looked desperate. "I don't know what to do. I really don't. But I couldn't just leave her there. She probably would have ended up dead."

"Well, guess what? You decided to be her knight in shining armor; now you're responsible for her. And let's talk about the real problem. She's having a baby. And she's your wife."

"Fuck." Bryce ran a hand through his shaggy hair. "You're not helping me here."

"What am I supposed to do? You created this whole mess, not me. Weren't there places you could have taken her, where she could have gotten help?"

He gave her a bleak look. "No. There was no place that would have been safe for her. The people who would be willing to take her off the streets would have been putting her in a whorehouse. And her baby would have lived in terrible circumstances. The children of Americans are considered outcasts; they're called things like half-breeds. You've never seen anything like it was over there."

GG's heart softened a little. She was sure he was telling the truth about that. She sat there for a minute and then laid her hand on her brother's. "Okay. I think we should sit down with Mom and Dad and talk this all out. Maybe if we all talk it over, we can come up with an idea that would work."

Bryce gripped her hand hard. "You really think so?"

"I think there's a lot better chance of coming up with something sensible if we're all trying to figure it out. I'll call Mom and figure out when we can all get together and I'll let you know. You're still at the Inn, right?"

"Yeah." His smile was bleak. "I don't really have anyplace else to go right now, either."

"The Inn is very nice. Quit feeling sorry for yourself."

Bryce had to laugh. "You're okay, sis. Isn't that boy awake yet?"

"No, he just went to sleep right before you got here. He was quite cranky, so I'm not waking him up."

Bryce kissed her on the top of the head. "Okay, I don't blame you. Listen, thanks for everything, really."

"Just out of curiosity, what does Carl have to say about all this?"

"Oh, just that I'm a real dumbass and I should have stuck to my policy of keeping things light and never serious."

"Hmm. He had a point."

Chapter 13

I t was quite a family meeting, as it turned out. Leo stayed home with James, a little relieved to have a good reason to stay out of this gathering. Bryce told his parents and Carl everything he had told GG, and his mother, especially, was as horrified as GG had been. Don was the only one who didn't find the story to be really surprising.

"I've read quite a bit about all the babies who have been born over there to Vietnamese mothers and American fathers. It's pretty ugly. The girls are outcasts and the children are even worse. Bryce is right; they call them half-breeds and children of the dust. A lot of babies are dropped off at orphanages or thrown in the trash because their mothers are terrified of being attacked by the Communist government. I can't say that marriage was the best way to handle this, but I don't blame you for feeling like you had to rescue her, son."

Margot said helplessly, "But what do we do now?"

Carl finally spoke up. "Look, let's figure out what the facts are and what we can and can't change. First, they're already married. That's done."

Bryce said, "Well, to be honest, it could be annulled."

They all stared at him until Carl snickered and said, "Okay, married but not consummated."

"Carl!" his mother said.

Carl shrugged and grinned. "Like I said, let's face what the facts are. Can you find the father, bro?"

"Probably. I'm an investigative reporter and he's in the Army. Shouldn't be all that hard. It was different before I got back here; it should be fairly simple now that I'm here."

"Okay. It seems fair to say that he should be found and informed that he's going to be a father. You're pretty confident that he wasn't going to go back for her, but it's still possible, right?"

Bryce said, "True. Then what do I do if he doesn't want to have anything to do with her?"

"Well, I guess she should know that," Carl said. "Does she still love him?"

"I think she does, but I also think she's lost her confidence that he loves her. She hasn't asked me to look for him since we got here."

GG said, "She's probably afraid to find out."

"So, when is the baby due?"

Bryce said, "End of October, give or take a little."

"And you're going to have to go back to work soon, am I right?" Carl was making a list of all the facts.

"Yeah, they want me back and they're offering me a couple of choices. If I don't make one soon, I'm going to lose that chance."

"And are these choices stateside?" Carl asked.

"Nope. Since Vietnam, they want me in hot spots. And I can't afford to turn them down."

"First of all, you need to find the father fast. Everything will depend on what he says. And next, we figure out what she should do. You can't just go off to a war zone somewhere and leave her. You brought her here, so you've at least got to put her in a safe place where she'll have the help she needs. And I assume she's on your health insurance, am I right?"

Bryce said glumly, "Yeah, you're right."

Margot snapped at him, "Bryce Devereaux, don't you act like you're getting roped into something you didn't want. This was all your doing, remember? Now, you owe that girl something. Not the rest of your life, but you owe her a start to a life of her own."

Bryce looked at his dad, who shrugged and said, "Your mother's right."

Bryce sat up a little straighter and said, "Okay. I can find the father, maybe even tomorrow. I'll have to get hold of him and tell him how things are. If he's in love with her, my dilemma might be over, but I don't think that's going to be the case. So then I have to find a safe place for Quyen to live and someone to help her through having the baby. And I have to get back to work. That's not negotiable."

GG said, "So you're going to be working on that tomorrow? Finding the father?"

"Yeah, I need to get it done fast."

"Then why don't you bring Quyen over to spend the day with me? That would be better than leaving her to just sit in a room at the Inn all day."

Her brother gave her a tired smile. "That would be really nice, sis. I'd appreciate it."

GG said briskly, "I'm not doing it for you, I'm doing it for her and her baby."

"I still appreciate it."

Don said, "Okay, son, you do that and your mother and I will talk it all over and see if we can come up with any constructive ideas. Call as soon as you find out something, and then we'll all get together again."

"All right." Bryce looked around at his family and said, "I really appreciate this more than you guys know."

Margot said, "Well, we know that you did it for good reasons, even if it wasn't the brightest thing you've ever done."

It was early afternoon when Bryce called to report that he'd found the father. He'd been discharged and was living back in his home town of Kansas City, Missouri. Bryce had gotten a phone number, and when he called the man and broke the news to him, the reaction was pretty much what he had expected. The guy said he had no idea what Bryce was talking about, he'd never been involved with a Vietnamese girl, and he was highly insulted at the suggestion that he had been. He had some ugly names to call the local girls there and said he'd never be caught dead with his dick in one. And besides all that, he was happily married with a baby on the way.

Bryce said grimly, "It's a good thing for you that we're having this conversation on the phone and not in person. You know what you did and you never had any intention of keeping your promises to her, did you?"

"Screw her. She spread her legs for somebody and she's just trying to get an American G.I. to take care of her and her kid. Sounds like she stuck you with her problem. Sorry for your luck. Don't call me again." And with that, he hung up.

Bryce swore and hung up the phone. He ran his hand through his hair, dreading telling Quyen about the conversation. Now, he was talking to his dad, who was disgusted at the reaction of the "man" who had left Quyen high and dry.

"Son, you're going to have to tell Quyen. You probably want to do that privately, don't you?"

Bryce said, "Yeah. She's very proud and she won't want this discussed with other people."

"All right. Then I'd say you should pick her up and take care of that as soon as possible. And once she can handle it, you two come over here and we'll discuss what we came up with. Let me know when you're coming and I'll get GG here." Don was quietly authoritative.

"Okay, Dad, thanks. I'll go get her now."

It was a good three hours later when the family gathered at the Devereaux home. Quyen had clearly been crying, but she was calm and composed as they sat together. Margot smiled gently at her and patted her hand.

"We've talked a lot about your situation and we think we have a solution," Don said. "Quyen, we'd like you to stay with us while you wait for your baby to be born. Bryce has to take an assignment and we've got plenty of room here."

Quyen's eyes were wide and uncomprehending. She looked at Bryce and he talked quietly to her in Vietnamese, such as it was. Then, in spite of herself, his wife's eyes filled with tears and she said something softly to him.

"She says it's too much kindness; she doesn't deserve it."

Margot said, "Nonsense. We want to do it. We want to make sure that you get the proper care and your baby is born healthy and strong."

GG said, "You can have my room; we'll fix it up for you. It'll be fun and it hasn't been that long since I had James, so I can help you."

Quyen faltered as she said, "I don't know what to say. You are giving me something my own family did not give me."

"Quyen, you didn't do anything wrong, but your family doesn't understand. And my guess is that they were afraid for you and your child. We can help you and it's only right that we do so," Don said kindly but firmly.

She looked anxiously at Bryce and asked, "Is it really all right?"

Bryce grinned at her. "It is. This is my family and this is how they are."

Quyen looked at all of them and smiled with a little glow in her eyes. "You have a very special family."

Bryce nodded. "I do. I'm very lucky to have them."

"I am sorry to bring shame to them," she said.

Margot said, "You were not the one who brought shame. The man who lied to you is the one who brought shame. And he only brought it on himself. You are not to worry about it anymore. What you have to do now is take good care of yourself, because that is taking good care of your baby."

"I know how to take care of babies. There were always babies in my village. I will take good care of my baby."

Margot smiled. "I'm glad to know that. And we'll help you."

GG said, "That's right; we will."

Bryce said, "I'll get hold of my news group tomorrow. I have to take an assignment; they're getting tired of waiting for me."

"Try to make it someplace a little safer than Vietnam," his mother said tartly.

"I'll see what I can do, Mom." Bryce grinned at her.

GG said, "Okay, let's get things ready as quickly as we can so that Quyen will be in a safe place when they send Bryce off to work."

"I don't see any reason why Quyen can't move over here tomorrow evening. We don't have to do much, just freshen up the room a little," Margot said.

"I'll come over tomorrow and help," GG said.

And so they had a plan. Bryce's mom wasn't happy with the news that he was going to the Gaza Strip but that was his assignment and he had to admit that he was excited about it. In just days, he was on his way to the Mideast and Quyen was comfortably settled into GG's room. The whole family did their best to make her feel comfortable and they quickly grew fond of her. GG introduced her to Katie and Sharon, and Quyen was shyly delighted to have friends. Dr. Harper was a little worried about the lack of proper nutrition she had had while in the early part of her pregnancy in Vietnam. Margot was constantly urging her to eat well and get plenty of rest along with reasonable exercise. She and GG were both a little concerned about her; she was thinner than she should be and she didn't just tire easily, she was tired all the time. She missed Vietnamese food and found American food hard to get used to, so Margot made sure that there was always plenty of fresh vegetables and fruit, and Quyen had rice every day.

In August, Dr. Harper said that Quyen was not gaining enough weight and needed to make an effort to gain a few pounds. Margot and Don discussed ways to get her to eat more and so Don went to Indianapolis one day and returned with an assortment of foods and treats from a Vietnamese market there. Quyen was overwhelmed with delight and gratitude, and she rationed the familiar foods to last as long as possible. She perked up and smiled more for a couple of weeks and Don decided that it would be well worth it to go again, this time with a list from Quyen. She was so excited at the prospect of getting another supply of foods that were familiar to her, that she glowed.

"If Papa Don can get me what I need, I can make Pho for the whole family," Quyen promised. "You will all love it."

GG looked intrigued. "What is it, Quyen? I never heard of it here in southern Indiana."

"It is a soup. So delicious, everybody is happy when someone makes Pho. It takes all day to prepare. But always worth it."

Margot got the beef bones and sirloin from Vance's and Don brought back everything else from Indianapolis, and the next day, Quyen made Pho. GG and Margot were fascinated with what she was doing. They watched and helped with what they could. That evening, when they all sat down to eat, they were happy to agree with Quyen that it was delicious. GG had carefully written down the recipe and notes of how the dish was made, and she would keep it for the rest of her days.

Quyen was happier for a period of time, but she still didn't gain enough weight. Dr. Harper was becoming concerned. He spoke to GG while Quyen got dressed after her doctor's appointment.

"The baby's heartbeat is strong and the baby is only slightly smaller than average for this point of the pregnancy. It's Quyen who concerns me. The baby is getting what he needs and Quyen is paying the price. Anything you can do to help her gain a little will help. It seems like the baby is thriving and Quyen is failing. I hate to see her go into labor that way; she won't have enough strength. If milkshakes every day will help her gain weight, or mashed potatoes, so be it."

They all tried to get Quyen to eat more, coaxing her to have a little extra of this or that. She was seeing the doctor every two weeks, and when she had gained two pounds at her next visit, he was encouraged, but he told them not to let up. At her next appointment, she had gained one more pound and Dr. Harper was clearly disappointed. But it was better than not gaining anything, so he smiled reassuringly at her and told her to keep eating and to remember that she was eating for two.

In early October, Quyen went into labor, three weeks early. Her labor was long and difficult and the family waited anxiously in the hospital waiting room. GG and Margot were in the labor room with Quyen, helping her breathe, holding her hand, sponging her forehead with a damp cloth, and encouraging her constantly. As the labor went on into the night, Quyen grew weaker and Dr. Harper looked more and more serious. Finally, long after midnight, the baby's head crowned. Quyen was wheeled into the delivery room and after what seemed like forever, a nurse hurried out to tell them the baby had been delivered.

"It's a boy; he's six pounds, two ounces and perfectly healthy. I've got to get back in there." The nurse hurried off and GG and Margot stared at each other, worried about Quyen.

More than an hour went by and then the nurse came back out. "I'm sorry, the little mother is having problems. They're working on her, trying to get her bleeding stopped, but she's very weak. Dr. Harper will talk with you as soon as he can."

When Dr. Harper finally came out, he looked exhausted. He said, "I'm so sorry. We did everything we could, but we couldn't get the bleeding stopped and she was just too weak. She put everything into having that baby; there just wasn't anything left for her."

GG and Margot were weeping in each other's arms and Don and Carl put their arms around the women, trying to comfort them. GG asked, "The baby? Is the baby all right?"

Dr. Harper nodded. "The baby's perfect. Poor Quyen just wasn't strong enough. If she hadn't had the bleeding problem, she would have had a chance, but even perfectly healthy women don't survive that kind of bleeding sometimes. I'm sorry. She would have been a wonderful mother."

"Can we see her?" Margot asked.

"They're getting her cleaned up and moving her out of the delivery room; then you can. Would you like to see the baby while they do that?"

GG wiped her tears away and said, "Yes, I'd like that."

He led them to the nursery and they looked through the window at the new babies. Quyen's baby was wrapped in a soft blue blanket and he was looking solemnly around as if he was taking in his surroundings. Then his little face twisted and he let out a cry, waving his little fists and working into a real scream. The nurse came over and picked him up, rocking him gently and offering him a bottle after making a notation on the clipboard hanging from his little bed. It took him a moment, but soon he was sucking greedily at the little bottle she held.

After they watched the baby for a while, Dr. Harper took

them back to see Quyen. Tears poured silently down GG's face as she took Quyen's hand. She looked as if she was peacefully asleep and GG grieved for the time she would never have with her son. "Poor baby. His mama is gone and his father wants nothing to do with him. It's just not fair. I'm so sorry, Quyen."

It was nearly dawn when they dropped GG off at home. Leo had taken James home hours earlier and put him to bed. GG waved wearily at her family as she let herself into the house. She went to the kitchen and put some water on for tea, then she turned and walked straight into Leo's arms when he walked into the room. He held her close, afraid to ask.

"She had a boy. He's beautiful; six pounds, two ounces and perfectly healthy. But Quyen… she started bleeding and they couldn't stop it."

"Oh God, GG." Leo's arms tightened around her.

"She didn't make it, Leo. She just… that poor baby. He's an orphan." GG sobbed in her husband's arms. "What's going to happen to him?"

Leo gathered her into his lap and rocked her. "I don't know, baby, but we'll figure it out."

He held her until she cried herself to sleep and then carried her off to bed.

Chapter 14

Bryce was only able to come back to the States for three days when Quyen was laid to rest. They put her in the Devereaux family plot with a stone that read "Quyen, Family For Too Short a Time." They had a little celebration of life for her at the Devereaux home. Sharon and Jack came, and Katie and Tommy did too. After a while, GG needed to get away from the sadness and she drew her two best friends outside with her.

"Thanks, you two. It was getting to where I couldn't breathe in there. It's just so sad. I didn't even think women died having babies anymore."

Katie gave her a hug. "It still happens. Not often, like it did in the old days, but it still does."

Sharon said, "What's going to happen to the baby?"

"I don't know. Right now, Mom is taking care of him, but that can't go on for much longer. Bryce says if he lets the Vietnamese authorities know, they'll demand that the baby come back to Vietnam. He doesn't have a chance at any kind of a good life there. They're terrible to kids like him there. They call them half breeds and children of the dust." GG was horrified all over again at the idea.

Katie looked horrified too. "That's terrible! He's just a baby; he didn't do anything wrong."

Sharon shook her head. "That's really awful. He can't go back there."

"We just haven't had time to figure anything out. But Bryce has to go back to the Mideast day after tomorrow. He's not much help."

"Can I tell you something?" Katie looked like she was barely holding on to a secret.

"Of course. Especially if it's something good," GG said with a little smile.

"Tommy and I are getting married."

"Oh, Katie, that's fantastic news!" GG threw her arms around her friend and Sharon put her arms around both of them.

There was a little babble of excited conversation and repeated congratulations. "When? What can we do to help?"

Katie laughed at them. "We're not having a wedding, to speak of. We're just going to go before a judge and get it done. But I would love for you both to be there with me."

GG said, "You couldn't keep me away if you tried. Are you sure you don't want a wedding, with your friends and family?"

"No, there's just Mom, and she doesn't approve. And Billy, who knows where he is?"

"My family would be there for you two," Sharon said.

"We know that, and we love you all. But you know Tommy. He's definitely not into ceremony and lots of people."

Sharon sighed. "You're right. I'm so happy for you two. Tommy hardly shows how he feels about things, but he's happy with you."

Katie gave her a quiet smile. "We're good together. We

have our scars, and we support each other; it's like we know when we need to give each other that support."

"I love you. And now you're really going to be my sister." Sharon hugged her hard.

"Hey, I want to be a sister too," GG complained.

Katie laughed and hugged her, too. "I wouldn't have it any other way."

"When is this happening?" Sharon asked.

"I'm not sure. We have to make an appointment at the courthouse."

GG said suddenly, "Katie, Mac could perform your ceremony. Remember, he got ordained so he could do it for some of the patients at the VA hospital?"

"Oh, GG, that's a great idea! I would love for Mac to perform our wedding. I'm going to talk to Tommy about it right away." Katie was thrilled at the idea.

Sharon said, "He'll love it."

"I'm so happy for you two," GG said. "I need to go check on James and see if Mom needs some help."

They went back inside the house, where Margot was just finished feeding the baby. James was still sleeping and Katie eagerly took the baby so that Margot and GG could do some things in the kitchen. Katie cuddled the tiny boy on her shoulder, patting his back and waiting for a burp. GG told her mother about Katie and Tommy, and Margot said, "Oh, that's lovely news. They're such a good couple. Just look at her; she looks so natural, holding that little one on her shoulder."

GG said thoughtfully, "She does, doesn't she?"

She went over to her friend and asked, "Do you need a break? I can take him if you do."

Katie said quickly, "Oh, no, I'm fine. He's just so sweet. It breaks my heart that he has no parents."

"I know. I don't know what's going to happen to him."

"They won't really send him back to Vietnam, will they?"

GG said, "We can't let that happen. Somehow, we've got to keep him here."

Bryce joined them and took the baby's tiny hand, gently stroking the little fingers. "He's so little. I'm afraid to hold him; he might break."

Katie laughed softly at him. "He's tougher than you think. He's not going to break."

"You look like you know what you're doing," Bryce said.

"I'm a nurse. I've had plenty of practice. How are you going to keep him from being sent to Vietnam?"

"Well, nobody there knows anything about him, so that's not really the problem. The problem is he needs a family and he doesn't have one. James just turned one and GG has her hands full with him. Mom can't raise a baby now; she's raised her family. I know Mom and GG both would keep him before they'd let him go to Vietnam, but that doesn't make it a good solution. I know a guy who could get an adoption done that would hold up here if I had a family for him. I need to find one, but I'll be gone the day after tomorrow."

"I wish I could just keep him," Katie said.

GG stared at her. "Katie…"

Her friend's eyes widened. Bryce stared at both of them as Katie said, "Do you think…"

"What?" Bryce was lost as they seemed to be communicating with each other without words. "What's going on?"

GG said, "Katie and Tommy are getting married."

Completely confused, Bryce said, "Congratulations, that's great."

"I need to talk to Tommy," Katie said.

"Yes. I'll go find him," GG said. She hurried off and returned a few minutes later with Tommy in tow.

"What's going on?" Tommy asked, then he saw Katie cuddling the baby. His face softened immediately and he said, "Look at you. Who have you got there? Wow, he's so little."

Katie turned the baby so he was cradled in her arms and Tommy bent his head over the tiny baby, holding his little hand and marveling at how small he really was. "Want to hold him?" she asked.

"Sure." Tommy didn't even hesitate. He took the baby and rocked him gently.

There were tears in GG's eyes as she watched them with the tiny, dark-haired child. Bryce met her eyes and he smiled and dared to hope that they'd found the family they needed. Katie said softly to GG, "We'll talk."

GG gave her a radiant smile.

By the time Bryce left Boone, the lawyer he'd contacted had the adoption in the works. If anyone had seriously challenged it, there could have been problems, but there was nobody who knew or cared anything about the child to raise any objections. The only ones who cared about the little, orphaned boy were right there in Boone, and none of them were anything but happy about the adoption. With the exception of Katie's mother, who didn't approve of anything, but she also wouldn't do anything that would cause her daughter trouble. Sometimes GG thought that her disapproval was only out of habit and that she used it as a mask to hide her real feelings. If she caught a look at Katie's mother when she wasn't aware of being watched, GG could see the little spark of pride on her face. Maybe she would soften in time.

Time flew by, birthdays and holidays were celebrated, and suddenly, it was time for James to start school. Leo took the morning off work on his son's first day of school and he and GG both stood with James, waiting for the big yellow school bus to stop at the end of their driveway. They had bought a slightly larger house on a couple of acres, where James could run and play outside with his dog and the neighbor's boy, who had quickly become James' best friend. They watched their son climb up into the big bus, where he turned and grinned at them as he waved. He had wanted to start school for months and he was more than eager to go. As soon as the bus pulled away, GG dissolved into tears and Leo held her close, a little choked up himself.

"He looked so little getting up into that big thing," GG said, swiping at her tears.

"And thrilled to death," her husband reminded her.

"He did," she admitted. "I'm glad he was excited about it, not nervous."

"He's going to be just fine. Now, I've got the whole rest of the morning off work; what should we do?" He gave her a wink and a leer.

GG laughed. "I don't know, but we'd better go in the house if it's what I think you have in mind."

She scampered to the house ahead of him and he followed with a chuckle. He did a good job of taking her mind off her son's first day of school over the next couple of hours.

After Leo went to work, GG baked a batch of cookies to celebrate with James later that afternoon. When she was finished, she sat down with a book she had been reading, but she couldn't get interested and finally laid it down and sat there reflecting over the last few years. Sharon and Jack had gotten married and finished school. They lived in Indianapolis, where they both had successful careers in their early stages. Katie and Tommy were happily married and raising their son, Danny, who was a sunny, sturdy little boy who made everyone smile. Even Katie's mother, in spite of herself, had fallen in love with him and doted on him like a true grandma. Carl had gotten engaged the year before, to a lovely woman they all loved, and would be married in the spring. And Bryce was still traveling the world, reporting the news. He had made quite a name for himself and was sent to the most important and dangerous locations, but he seemed to thrive on it. He left broken hearts wherever he went and had kept his vow to keep things light, never serious.

It occurred to GG that with James in school, she was going to have a lot more time on her hands. She would enjoy it at first, but she knew it would quickly get old. She thought about the last time she had gotten bored because she had too much time on her hands and had to laugh. This time, she would find herself something to do. Maybe it was time to have a job again. The little gift shop she had worked at before was still there and still owned by the same woman. She decided to stop in and talk to her soon. But for now, she was going to make her son's favorite dinner to celebrate his first day of school.

At the end of the week, Leo came home from work with a funny look on his face. He kissed his wife and tossed James in the air, making him laugh breathlessly, and GG wondered what was on his mind. He didn't say anything until they sat down to dinner.

"Some things are happening at work that we need to talk about," Leo said as he sliced off a bite of his roast beef.

"What's going on?" GG asked.

"Well... I had a call from another firm. They were offering me a job, and it's a good one."

"Have you been looking at other jobs? I thought you loved it where you are."

"No, I haven't made any inquiries. But it turns out they called to check to see if Baxter and Stone would have an objection to them approaching me, and they gave them the okay. They said they don't want to lose me, but they wouldn't stand in my way if I wanted to make a move."

GG was impressed. "That's kind of a big deal, isn't it?"

James asked, "Are you getting a new job, Daddy?"

"Just talking about it, son. Yeah, it's kind of flattering. It took me by surprise." Leo was a little hesitant.

"So are you interested in it?" GG asked.

"Well, it's not that simple. I'd have to talk to them, find out a lot more about the job. They're a larger firm, so there would be more opportunities for advancement, but there would also be more competition. It would be a lot different than where I am now, more pressure, I'm sure. And it's in Colorado."

GG looked stunned. "Colorado? That's... that's so far away."

"I know." Leo was watching her closely.

"But do you *want* to move that far away?"

Leo's expression was neutral. "It's beautiful there. There's a lot to do, with the mountains, the parks, skiing, horses, hiking. James is young; he'd adapt quickly, I'm sure."

"You sound like you're excited about it."

"It's not all about me; it would affect all of us. I haven't even told them that I'd talk to them about it. I told them I had to talk to my family first."

GG didn't know what to think. The idea of moving away from both their families and all their friends was overwhelming, but did she have a right to stand in his way if this was what he wanted? "Well, what do you want to do, Leo? Do you want to talk to them more?"

Leo was firm. "I'm not deciding this based on just what I want. We're a family. This is about all of us, and I'm not making any kind of a decision without you."

"I don't know what to say, Leo; I really don't."

"I'd like to go to the mountains," James piped up.

They both laughed and Leo winked at him. "Don't worry, you'll get to see mountains. We don't have to move there to make that happen."

"And the ocean," his mother said. "It's time for you to start seeing the world, James."

Leo nodded. "It is. We've been so busy building our lives here that we've kind of forgotten about that. I promised you that we'd travel and see the world."

GG said thoughtfully, "You did, but I don't feel like I've been missing out on anything. But we should show James more than just Boone."

"Let's think about the whole job offer thing and also start planning a family vacation."

GG nodded. "Let's do that."

"I don't think we can afford Europe, though."

GG laughed. "There's plenty to see right here in the U.S.."

Leo said, "There sure is. Maybe we should get a camper."

James looked thrilled. "Seth has a camper! I want to go camping. Seth goes all the time, and he has lots of fun."

Leo gave him a grin. "Then let's do it."

"Leo! Buying a camper…"

He laughed. "I'm not jumping into anything. We can rent a camper for our first trip; try it out and see if we like it."

GG looked relieved. "Okay, that makes sense. Yeah… yeah, that could be fun."

"James, did you know that your mom slept out on the ground under the stars one time?"

James stared at his mom, his eyes wide. "You did?"

GG nodded solemnly. "I did. Aunt Sharon and me. We slept under the stars in sleeping bags."

"Wow, Mom, what was it like?"

GG looked dreamy. "It was beautiful. There were millions of stars, and the night was just right, with a little breeze. And we could hear little bits of music coming from different places, where people were still up, sitting around their campfires."

"There were lots of people there?"

"Yeah, it was like a really big camp out."

"That's so neat! Where was I? And where was Dad?"

"That was before your dad and I really got to know each

other. And you weren't born yet. Dad and I weren't even boyfriend and girlfriend yet."

"Geez, Mom, you did cool things!" James was deeply impressed.

Leo laughed. "She did a lot of cool things, son. More than anybody could keep track of."

GG shot him a look, laughing. "Hush. You're going to get to do a lot of cool things, James."

Her son looked thrilled. "I can't wait to go camping. Can we take Rebel? Seth takes his dog."

Leo said, "Sure. That's part of going camping."

Later that night, GG lay with her head on Leo's shoulder and tried to get him to talk more about the job offer. Frustrated, she finally asked, "Why won't you tell me how you really feel about it? Is it something you want?"

"Because I need to know how you really feel about it. You've always wanted to see more of the world, go more places. This would be a chance to do that. I promised you that you wouldn't be stuck in Boone your whole life. I promised you that I would show you more of the world."

GG propped herself up on her elbow and stared at him. "Is that what this is all about? Leo Beauchamp, that was when I was a *teenager*, for heaven's sake! We have a home here, family and friends, and a life. I don't want to uproot all that, not unless you're going after something you really want or need. If that's the case, I'll go anywhere with you. You and James are my life now. I'm not a teenager anymore."

Leo swept her into his arms and squeezed so hard that she squealed. Nuzzling her neck, he said, "I am so happy to hear you say that. I'm happy where I am, but I didn't want to keep you from all your dreams. You had so many and you gave them up to marry me. I love you more than I ever knew you could love someone, and I just want you to be happy."

GG's kiss was long and tender. "Don't you know how

happy I am? I have everything here. I don't have to see the world to know that. You didn't take away my dreams; you just changed them. Now they're all coming true, right here."

Leo lowered his head to kiss her deeply. They made slow, sweet love long into the night and slept in each other's arms.

Chapter 15

L eo and GG kept their promise to James; they didn't show him the whole world, but they did a good job of exploring the U.S. They ended up buying a camper and used it often, taking a two-week vacation every summer so they could travel greater distances. Sometimes they brought a friend along for James and on several shorter, weekend trips, Tommy and Katie let them take Danny. Eventually, they bought a camper of their own and the two couples traveled together fairly often. They saw lakes, mountains, deserts, caves, state parks and forests, and the ocean, of course. James learned to love the outdoors, but when he got a little older, sports became his passion and GG learned to grit her teeth when he took a big hit on the football field or came down hard on the basketball court.

GG went back to work part time in Lydia's gift shop and kept right on taking arts and crafts classes, not for her own creativity, but for the talented people she met there. Leo became a senior engineer in his firm and volunteered twice a month to work with a group that created plans for improvements in crumbling neighborhoods; their plans were then implemented by a volunteer construction group. Both of them were busy following James' sports events and supporting his teams. They helped load equipment for away games and participated in all the activities that took place, to help the teams pay for their uniforms, summer camps, and all the other various expenses that never were fully paid for by the school.

By the beginning of James' junior year, it was obvious that he wanted to go away to college. He worked hard to keep his grades up and he was an accomplished athlete. GG fretted over the idea of having him go away at such a young age, but remembering how badly she had wanted to get out of Boone, she knew she couldn't stand in his way. He wasn't talking about running off to live in a commune in California; he was talking about going away to a good college to get a good education. He began visiting colleges the second half of his junior year and they visited with him, seeing the campuses with their own eyes. By the time he started his senior year, he had his heart set on MIT, where he planned to study aerospace engineering. And when he was accepted, he was eager to see his dreams come true.

GG and Leo gave their full support to their son, knowing that he was serious about his plans and dedicated to working as hard as he could to be successful. They had a graduation party for him, and the entire family and all their friends gathered to celebrate with him. They offered to give him a trip for his graduation present, but James told them he'd rather have them put the money into helping him get started in his college life. And so, that was what they did. They saw him off to school and made sure he had everything he needed to get started. And after they left him there, they started the long trip back home with the emptiness echoing around them. After driving for an hour, Leo suddenly cursed out loud and pulled off the freeway and into a rest stop. As soon as he gathered his wife into his arms, she burst into tears and he rocked her and comforted her, a few tears of his own mingling with hers.

Finally, GG wiped her tears away and gave a shaky little laugh. "I knew it would be hard, but I had no idea what it would actually feel like. It's like he's gone forever."

Leo admitted, "I didn't think it would feel like this. He's been away from home before, off to sports camp and things like that, but this time it seems so final."

"But did you see his face? Did you see how happy he was? He didn't even seem one little bit nervous! And his roommate seemed like a really nice kid. They were talking a blue streak when we were driving away."

Leo grinned. "I did see it. It looks like he's where he really belongs. He's going to work his ass off there, you can just tell. He's not about to waste the opportunity he's got."

"Oh, Leo, I'm so proud of him. But I miss my baby. It seems like we just had him yesterday and now he's all grown up."

"He's still your baby; he always will be. And we can't stop him from growing up."

"I know. And I know it was the best thing we could do, to support him in what he's doing. He's so serious about it. He knows just how hard it's going to be, and he's looking forward to it. It just makes me proud."

Leo kissed her and said, "It makes me proud too. And, to be honest, it's going to be kind of nice to have you all to myself for a while. I can make love to my wife and make all the noise I want to now…"

GG laughed. "I guess that's true. We won't have to keep it to a whisper anymore, will we?"

"Mm," Leo murmured as he nuzzled her neck. "I think I need to get you home."

When they pulled back into traffic, they both felt better. And the days just ahead of them were going to be busy.

Leo's sisters had both moved out of the house and his parents had finally decided that they wanted to move where it was warm and sunny. They had bought a place in a Florida retirement community, where they could socialize and play golf to their hearts' content without worrying about lawn work and cold weather. Leo and GG were moving into the family home in Boone and they had promised to always keep it in the family. By Halloween, Charles and Claire had completed their move to their new home and Leo and GG were putting the final touches on theirs. GG knew it was going to take her a while to get used to the size of the house, but she knew it well and had always loved it.

After dinner one night, Leo helped his wife load the dishwasher and then pulled her against him. He wrapped his arms around her and kissed her until she melted against him and gave a throaty, little moan of desire. "Did you ever think this would be home?" he asked.

"No," GG murmured.

"Remember when we made love for the first time in our first home of our own? That cramped, little rental house. But it was our home."

GG chimed in, "And we loved it. We were happy there until we had James and it was time to have more room."

"And now, look. We have this great big place all to ourselves. It's kind of weird, but Mom and Dad are right. I can't imagine not keeping this house in our family. There's just too much history in it."

"It's going to be great when we have family here for holidays, or just to get together. And someday, James will have a wife and children. Can you imagine having grandchildren?" GG had clearly thought about it before.

Leo laughed. "Hey, we're not old enough for that yet. Besides, I want to enjoy some time alone with my wife. No more awards dinners or bake sales to raise money for new jerseys."

"You're going to miss all that and you know it." But when Leo cupped her bottom in his hands and squeezed, she gave a breathless little squeal. "But, maybe you're right... maybe we need some time to ourselves." She reached up to kiss him, twining her hand in his hair and pulling him close.

Leo swept her up in his arms and carried her into the den, where he had laid a thick, furry throw on the floor in front of the fireplace and built a warm, crackling fire. He gently lowered her to the soft throw and stretched out beside her, kissing and stroking her, until her nerve endings tingled with little thrills of pleasure. He slowly unbuttoned her blouse, kissing her throat and the swell of her breasts, chuckling at her protest. "Don't worry, the doors are all locked."

And so GG sighed against his mouth and let the sensations take her. She slid her hands up under his sweater and stroked his hard, muscled belly while he finished undoing her buttons and slipped her blouse off her shoulders, to toss it aside and kiss her bare shoulder. With one hand, he undid her bra and pulled it off too. GG insistently tugged at his sweater until he obliged her and pulled it off over his head. She moaned when he held her close to him, her bare breasts against his bare chest, her sensitive nipples rubbing against him. He trailed a line of burning kisses down her throat and to the hollow between her breasts as he cupped them in his hands and slowly, teasingly lowered his mouth to them. His tongue darted out and lapped at one swollen, rosy tip and GG arched her back, wordlessly begging for more. But he kept up the teasing until she gasped and pulled his head to her. Finally, he closed his mouth over one lovely mound, licking and sucking at her nipple until she gasped with the electric sensations shooting down her spine.

GG felt the long, low pull in her belly and the heat

between her legs as moisture trickled there, leaving her panting for Leo's touch. She pulled at his belt, impatiently loosening his pants as he laughed at her and nipped her lightly. When she freed his hard length from the confining garments, she gave a little laugh of triumph and wrapped her hand around him. Now Leo was the one gasping in response to her touch and he undid her jeans and tugged them down and off, suddenly needing to have her fully bared to him. He stroked her soft skin and kissed her ribcage, then her belly, then the sensitive spot at the top of her thigh.

"Oh! God, Leo, please…" GG's legs fell open as his mouth traveled lower and he spread her open to his tongue. He feasted on her sweet, swollen center, his tongue exploring her most intimate places. He was pushing her relentlessly toward an orgasm, but she wanted him inside her and she begged him for it shamelessly. When he rose up and then lowered himself to her, she rose to meet him and he buried himself deep inside her. GG wrapped her legs around him and rose to meet his thrusts, crying out, again and again, as the pleasure grew more and more intense. It seemed impossible that it could be so overwhelming. The wave rose on and on as they rocked together in the driving rhythm of his thrusts until they finally exploded in spasms of orgasm, GG's strong contractions milking him and wringing a cry from him as they shuddered together, shaking with the aftershocks of pure pleasure.

They lay wrapped in each other's arms, until their breathing slowed and the sweat cooled on their bodies, and then basked in the warmth of the fire. The firelight flickered on their nakedness, and after a time, they began to murmur to each other, as they always had. They never seemed to run out of things to talk about, their plans, their families, the love they shared. It had grown deeper and deeper over the years, until sometimes they almost seemed to read each other's minds. Their goals were the same, the things that made them happy were the same, when they were worried about something, they supported each other. They had become as one in the satisfaction of their lives together.

"See?" Leo said. "We couldn't do this when James was at home."

GG laughed at him. "Well, no, we really couldn't. But we've had our share of private moments."

Leo laughed too, thinking back on some of those private moments. "Remember the time we were camping and James and Seth went to a class at the campground to learn to tie knots?"

"Yes, we barely managed to get our clothes on before they came running back to our campsite."

They were both laughing.

Leo said, "That was close."

GG said, "And the time we had twenty minutes before James got home to change so we could take him to football practice?"

"Yeah, and Seth's dad pulled up five minutes early and we were in the kitchen, not quite... finished."

GG was laughing hard. "I ran to the bathroom and you ducked into the pantry to get yourself presentable before he came through the front door. Do you think he ever suspected?"

"Maybe. But if he did, he sure didn't want to talk about it, did he?"

GG shook her head, still laughing. "It was bad enough that we were constantly embarrassing him by kissing any time we wanted to."

Leo laughed. "Oh, yeah, I forgot about that stage. He was constantly embarrassed by us for a year or so."

"He finally gave up on it after our only reaction was to laugh at him. Oh, Leo, it's going to be so hard not to have him here for Thanksgiving."

Leo gave her a squeeze. "It is, but he's right. He's just settling in and he's got a lot to get used to. If he thinks that he'd be better off using those quiet days to work on his classes, we've got to respect that. He'll be home for Christmas."

"That seems so far away. I miss making his favorite dinners and rustling up snacks for him and his friends. Heck, I even miss doing his laundry when he was too busy."

"I know, baby, it's hard to get used to him being gone."

"I'm glad we had moving to keep us busy when he first left. But just about everything is done now. Pretty soon, I'm going to be trying to find things to keep me busy. And... I just miss him."

Leo was listening and thinking. He knew she was right; it was going to be hard for her. He gave her a suggestive leer. "I'll keep you busy, darlin'."

GG snuggled against him. "I'll let you. But you have to go to work, you know. I'll figure it out. Everybody goes through this when their kids grow up."

But when GG was unhappy, Leo didn't like it. He thought about it constantly, determined to come up with a way to help her. And one day, he found a solution. A few days later, he came home from work in an unusually cheerful mood. GG was in the kitchen, baking yet another batch of cookies they didn't need. She had donated the last two batches to the church day care center. And she did her best to put on a cheerful front, but Leo knew that she still cried sometimes when she was alone. It made his heart ache for her and he was determined to do something about it.

"Are you about finished here?" Leo asked.

"Why? I've got one more sheet of cookies to bake."

"I need to take you for a ride."

"What for? It'll be dinnertime before you know it. And I've got this mess to clean up before I make dinner." GG wasn't thrilled with the idea.

"I'll wait until you're done in here. But as soon as the cookies are baked, we'll go."

GG said impatiently, "Go where, Leo? I'm in the middle of things here."

"Never mind where. Just finish what you're doing." He winked at her and went to change clothes, whistling as he went.

GG glared after him, unreasonably annoyed by his cheerfulness. She banged the pans in the kitchen as she finished up with the cookies, and when she took the last pan of cookies out, she went to find him. "Well, I'm done," GG said.

"Good." Leo gave her a quick kiss and reached around to untie her apron. "Go get your coat."

Exasperated, GG protested, "Leo, it's late. It's already starting to get dark. And it's cold outside. Why on earth do we have to go someplace now?"

He swatted her on the bottom and said, "Don't argue with me, wife. Go get your coat."

She huffed out a frustrated breath and went to get her coat. Leo opened his truck door for her and, whistling, went around to get in behind the wheel. He started the truck and then turned to her. "Now, I'm going to blindfold you so you don't see where we're going." He pulled a scarf out of his pocket and moved toward her.

"Oh, no, you're not. I don't know what you're up to, but this is not funny."

"Are you arguing with me again? You know what happens to wives who don't behave themselves. Now turn your head."

GG said, "You can't spank me for refusing to let you blindfold me."

Leo gave her an evil grin. "Wanna bet?"

"Ooh!" If she could have stamped her foot, she would have. Scowling, she turned so he could blindfold her with the scarf.

"Okay, here we go." He backed out of the driveway and started down the street, whistling cheerfully. GG didn't say a single word. After a few minutes of driving, Leo pulled the truck to a stop and said, "Sit still."

More frustrated than ever, GG sat and waited. He opened her door and helped her out, keeping her blindfolded. He led her for a few steps and then stopped. "Okay, we're here." He gently untied the scarf and pulled it away from her. GG blinked, looking around, and then said, "What are we doing here?"

"I've been thinking and thinking about how to make you feel better about the change in our lives, and I realized that you need something of your own to nurture. And, it turns out that Lydia has been wanting to retire."

GG shook her head in confusion. "Lydia has been wanting to retire? I know she talks about it once in a while, but it's just talk."

Leo took her hand. "No, it wasn't just talk. She really did want to retire. And it works out really well for all concerned."

"What do you mean, Leo?"

"I mean I bought the shop for you. It's all yours now, GG. It's yours to run, to expand, to improve... anything you want to do with it."

She stared at him in disbelief for a long minute, opened her mouth to talk, then closed her mouth and blinked as tears filled her eyes. She opened her mouth again and then burst into tears.

Aghast, Leo said anxiously, "GG, what's wrong? I thought you loved this shop."

"I do love it," GG sobbed through her words. "I just... I just can't believe you did this. Leo, you really did this for me?"

He wrapped his arms around her, and she cried on his shoulder. "GG, I'd do anything for you. Don't you know that? I'd do anything to make you happy."

GG sobbed harder. "Oh, Leo, I love you so damn much!"

He turned her hand over and pressed a set of keys into it. "Should we go in and look at your shop?"

"Yes! Yes. Oh, my word, I just can't believe this." She wiped at the tears and gave him a watery smile. He leaned down to kiss her, and they went to the door together so that GG could unlock the door to her own business for the very first time.

Chapter 16

GG found that owning the shop was her niche. She threw herself into cleaning up and giving it a fresh new look, and Leo was happy to help with whatever she needed. He completely redid the little bathroom for her, patched drywall, and put up the new light fixtures that his wife chose. She made him set her up with a shop budget and vowed that one day she would pay him back for the investment he had made. She hired Tommy's little company to rewire the whole shop and she put a fresh coat of paint on everything. Carl made her a new sign for the front of the shop, over the door, and she named it GG's Gems. She had no time to brood about her son moving off to college; she was busier than she had ever been in her life, it seemed.

James was thriving at college. He came home for Christmas and the family celebrated together with full hearts. James was determined to keep his grades up and he was fired up by the serious learning atmosphere that he had found at MIT. He was inordinately proud of his mother and her new business venture and he congratulated his dad for thinking of it. GG was tentatively planning a spring grand opening; once the remodeling was nearly finished, she had shifted her focus to finding local artisans to place their work in her shop. She loved finding them and talking to them and giving them the opportunity to sell their work and spread the word about their talents.

Boone was a picturesque place at Christmas time; the people of Boone loved decorating and celebrating Christmas, and many people drove through just to see the pretty little town at holiday time. GG was already looking forward to making the next Christmas a real event for her shop. On Christmas Eve, the family went to the candlelight service at the little church and on Christmas Day, all the family members who were still around Boone gathered at GG and Leo's home. Carl came with his wife and their two children and Bryce surprised them once again by showing up just before they sat down to dinner. It was a joyous celebration and GG thought she had never been so happy as she looked around the big table at the gathering of their families. When she had a quiet moment a little later, she called Sharon's house and, sure enough, Tommy and Katie were there along with Katie's mother. So, once they were finished there, Katie and Tommy stopped by the Beauchamps' with Danny, who had grown into a confident, outgoing young man.

Bryce was nearly overcome by emotion as he shook hands with Danny, who had been a baby when he'd seen him last. Tommy and Katie had always been open about how they had come to be Danny's parents and Danny was thrilled to meet Bryce. They sat for a long time talking and Katie watched them with a smile. GG put an arm around her friend and gave her a hug.

"It's good to see, isn't it?" GG asked.

"Oh, it is!" Katie was so proud of her son, and it showed.

"We've told him all the stories we could, and I don't know if you knew this, but a few years ago Danny wrote a letter to Bryce and they've been writing back and forth ever since."

GG was surprised and touched. "No, I didn't know that. That's wonderful. Bryce never mentioned it."

Katie gave a little laugh. "Men. They never volunteer very much, do they?"

"A lot of them don't. Now, Leo likes to talk about everything. But he kept it a complete surprise when he bought the shop for me."

"That was such a great thing to do. He did it because James was gone, didn't he?"

GG nodded. "He did. He always seems to know how I'm feeling, even when I don't say a word about it."

Katie gave her a hug. "You and Leo are the closest couple I know. It's like the two of you share one brain. You're just always on the same page."

GG laughed. "I don't know. We've had a few real battles. But we promised before we ever got married that we would not go to bed angry with each other, and we've done a pretty fair job of keeping that promise."

"Well, you two are meant for each other."

"I think I'd have to say the same for you and Tommy."

Katie gave her a radiant smile. "We've been good together. And Danny is the best thing that ever happened to us. When I think of that day you stood up for me at school, and what it turned out to be the beginning of…"

"It was meant to be. We've all been lucky here in Boone, haven't we? Oh, look, Sharon's here!"

Sharon swept across the room and the three women hugged each other, long and hard. Sharon and Jack had three sons and incredibly busy lives, but the three women had always stayed close and Leo and Jack were still close friends. In fact, the two of them were planning to take a short fishing trip together in the early summer. The house was full of family, friends, talk, and laughter just as GG had pictured it when they had moved in. And, as far as she was concerned, it had all come from loving Leo.

The End

Kat Carrington

Hi! I'm Kat Carrington and I write romance; sweet, spicy romance with happy ever after endings. I'm a grandmother and I'm having the time of my life letting my imagination go and telling the kind of stories that I like to read. And it's been a wonderful bonus to find out that other people like to read them too.

I was born and raised in Indiana where I raised my kids and welcomed the most amazing people into my life, my grandchildren. Having grandchildren is my greatest blessing. I'm living now in South Carolina with my always supportive hubby.

From the time I learned to read, there was always a book in my hands. After I consumed all the fiction in my elementary school library I moved on to biographies, which I found to be endlessly fascinating. Once I retired and we moved south I discovered that I was ready for a new venture. I thought back to when I was in fifth grade and sat for hours at a time at my dad's big desk writing stories with a pencil on notebook paper. One day I opened my laptop and started a story.

That first book took nearly two years to write. I'd write for a while, then forget all about it for a while. Somewhere along the way it changed from a whim to a real story that I had to finish. And that's when Blushing Books changed my whole life. My book was accepted for publication and was released on May 29, 2019. Writing is now part of my life and I hope you all enjoy my stories and the characters I keep falling in love with.

Don't miss these exciting titles by Kat Carrington and Blushing Books!

Dirty Politics
Crash and Burn

A Strong Man's Hand
Maggie's Match
Shelby's Secrets
Surviving Savannah
Boone Beginnings
Loving Leo

Dusty Dreams Ranch
Jessie's Dusty Dreams
A Dusty Dreams Wedding

Blushing Books

Blushing Books is the oldest eBook publisher on the web. We've been running websites that publish steamy romance and erotica since 1999, and we have been selling eBooks since 2003. We have free and promotional offerings that change weekly, so please do visit us at http://www.blushingbooks.com/free.

Blushing Books Newsletter

Please join the Blushing Books newsletter
to receive updates & special promotional offers.
You can also join by using your mobile phone:
Just text BLUSHING to 22828.

Every month, one new sign up via text messaging will receive
a $25.00 Amazon gift card, so sign up today!

www.ingramcontent.com/pod-product-compliance
Lightning Source LLC
Chambersburg PA
CBHW020647180626
46816CB00003B/1171